MATAMOROS MISSION

Thanks to a toy soldier's stupidity, the troopers with Anderson were shot to pieces before they even landed, leaving Anderson to swim for his life in the mangrove jungle. Hunted like an animal, he found friends where he hadn't expected them, and took on his enemies, the crooked banker Bradley Gill and Lee Sharrock, the black pistolero. Then came the most dangerous one of all, the man he'd come to find — Amarillo.

JEFF SADLER

MATAMOROS MISSION

Complete and Unabridged

LINFORD
Leicester

First published in Great Britain in 1993 by
Robert Hale Limited
London

First Linford Edition
published February 1995
by arrangement with
Robert Hale Limited
London

British Library CIP Data

Sadler, Jeff
    Matamoros mission.—Large print ed.—
Linford western library
I. Title II. Series
823.914 [F]

ISBN 0–7089–7691–3

Published by
F. A. Thorpe (Publishing) Ltd.
Anstey, Leicestershire
Set by Words & Graphics Ltd.
Anstey, Leicestershire
Printed and bound in Great Britain by
T. J. Press (Padstow) Ltd., Padstow, Cornwall

This book is printed on acid-free paper

For Mike Lineker
The troubleshooter and friend in
need who brought us safely to the
Groucho Club and back again

1

FIRST of the shots came at them as they neared the island, lashing from the thickets closest to the shore. Hunched behind the soldiers in the long pirogue, striking his own paddle deep as they headed for land, the earliest warning they gave him were the sudden columns of spray thrown up alongside as bullets struck the water. Ragged blast of the explosions came after, and gunflames stabbed through the murk and the heavy, sheeting rain. Anderson swore fiercely, bent to drive the paddle harder as smoke wreathed the bushes ahead, and the noise of gunshots echoed hollow across the water. Out here the bunch of them were sitting ducks. Only chance they had was to make for land.

Up ahead of them the island showed, its unsure outline looming through a hissing wall of rain. Anderson shook droplets of water from his eyes, his face and body soaked through from the downpour as he scanned the shoreline. Overgrown tangles of mangrove roots spilled down to the water's edge, thickening to form an impenetrable barrier for several yards inland. Higher above them, the green of other foliage sheathed the land, dense growths of brush and sparse trees combining to mask the waiting ambushers from sight. Across the huge expanse of swamp, deeper into the murk, he could just about make out the grey hummocked shapes of other islands, and beyond them the darker mass of mangrove jungle that ran clear to Matamoros and the coast. Anderson grimaced, wiping his sodden face with his sleeve.

Hell of a place to come to for the pleasure of getting himself shot.

Second volley whiplashed from the shore almost as he took in the sight, the warm air suddenly heavy with the whine of speeding bullets. Something hot and fast plucked close by Anderson's stubbled face, a faint breeze feathering his cheek as it passed. In front of him, the nearest of the *federales* grunted and swayed, keeling over to lose his paddle. Anderson caught a glimpse of the welling, fist-sized hole in his uniformed back in the moment before the dying soldier pitched across the side of the pirogue, and the boat wallowed out of control.

Caught in the open, away from the shore, the boats with their freight of federal troopers shuddered to a merciless, raking fire from the bush-whackers on the island. Heavy calibre bullets ripped into the frail pirogues, scything down the huddled shapes of the *federales*, holing the thin-skinned craft to let in the water from the swamp. Anderson saw an overturned boat rear keel-upwards in the water, heard the cries of men who floundered to stay afloat. Back of him a soldier lurched upright in the bed of the pirogue, yelling as he ploughed over to hit the water. Anderson fought to keep his balance as the boat leaned sideways and threatened to turn turtle, the dead *hombre* in front of him sliding head foremost into the swamp. He dug frantically with the paddle, trying to bring the craft around as fresh gunshots hammered through the downpour, and the dark swamp water lapped in to cover his feet.

Salazar's craft was lost to sight by now, hidden from him somewhere in the drenching murk. Anderson heard the harsh, bellowing voice of Aguirre as the officer tried vainly to rally his men. Some of the *federales* had thrown their paddles aside, hoisting their rifles to fire back at the gunflashes that lit the smoke-shrouded bushes on the island. Crouched aboard the unsteadily rocking boats, firing at unseen ambushers as their comrades were mown down about them, the Mexican soldiers didn't have a prayer. Successive volleys tore into them, cut the uniformed figures down in bloody swathes as the fragile pirogues yawed and overturned in the water. From around the far side of the island, other boats showed suddenly, heading towards them through the bucketing rain. Anderson saw the silhouettes of standing and seated figures in the pirogues as they lined carbines and pistols in readiness, firing without mercy at the uniformed shapes in the water.

He caught a momentary glimpse of Aguirre as the captain's boat drew up beside him. Face of the officer streamed blood from a gash above the eye, and his features were contorted in a soundless snarl of rage. Aguirre didn't seem to see him, his fierce gaze intent on the oncoming pirogues as he fired blindly into the rain with his service revolver. Cracking of other gunshots answered from the island, and a slug burned close above Anderson's head. The dark man flinched to the angry hornet-whine of the bullet, gritted his teeth as the shot ripped the battered Army campaign hat from his hair.

Anderson felt it flop between his shoulders, held in place only by the frayed cord that caught around his neck.

Beneath him the pirogue was already sinking, a dark tide rushing in through the holed keel to reach almost to his knees. The foremost trooper collapsed over the prow as the next volley hit raggedly from ashore, his arm trailing loose into the water. His companions were already overboard and swimming for their lives. Anderson felt the dying shudder run through the stricken boat and cursed, tossing his paddle aside. He flung himself clear as the pirogue filled and went under with a gurgling rush, diving headlong into the swamp.

Water was dark, thick and warm as molasses, littered with weeds and slimy half-seen growths. Anderson hit and went under, fought his way back to the surface in something close to a panic. Warm, humid spatters of rain struck at his face as he made it to air again, and the dark man spluttered, gulping it in.

He sleeved the black, swamp-plastered hair out of his eyes, peering into the heavy downpour. Shots still cracked from the island, and from the pirogues that nosed their way through the rain in search of swimming *federales*, but right now he couldn't make out any sign of Aguirre and the rest. The dark man scowled, turning his back on the stretch of water. Nothing to see back there, he reckoned. Wasn't nothing but a massacre, any way you called it.

He launched himself forward, striking powerfully in the direction of the shore. From behind him came a high, excited yelp, and a bullet whipped by him at heart-stopping speed. It hit the weedy surface close enough to throw spray into his face, but by then Anderson was already on his way underwater. The dark man made a fair distance before lack of air forced him to the surface again, and when he came up to breathe no one else was sending shots after him. Looked like he'd slipped them for the moment, at least.

7

Through a grey curtain of rain the rim of the island edged closer, last threads of gunsmoke drifting away above the bushes. He struck out towards it, aiming to work around the near side away from the bushwhackers and the *hombres* scouring the swamp in their pirogues, gasping in effort as the warm, thick water dragged on his body and fought to hold him back.

Somewhere back of him he heard the floundering splash of men in the water, and further into the distance other voices called harshly from the prowling boats in the swamp. Chances were they hadn't given up just yet, and were coming after to pick up on what was left. Anderson quickened his stroke, plunging forward strongly through the dark water, heading away from the smoke-hung shore to come in around the island on its near side.

Force of the rain eased off by a touch, the pelting wall of water shrinking gradually to a heavy shower of droplets that speckled the surface around him. Anderson hauled in close to the rim of the land, and followed it around the best way he could, hearing the breath rasp in his chest with every stroke. He'd covered a hell of a distance to get this far, and had managed to swallow a fair amount of water after the first dive. Inwardly he sensed he wouldn't be able to stay the pace much longer. Movement brought him into the shadow of the mangrove thickets that overhung the swamp, and the dark man spared them a brief sidelong glance. Seen from below, they struck him as impressive, and not a little daunting. Dense tangle of tough-barked bushes that stood maybe forty feet high in places, their roots hanging down to dip and anchor themselves in the mud beneath. Thick-leafed branches and crowns linked to form a jungle of hard, knotty wood that left barely an opening for a half-starved snake to get through, let alone a man. Anderson studied the trunks with their reddish-brown bark, the boughs with their glossy leaves and pale yellow flowers. No way into there, he thought.

Far behind him, the sound of splashing had quietened, but his keen ears caught the slam of a shot, and a high, wavering scream. Anderson sucked the breath into his lungs, and kicked out for a point further along the shore. For once, he'd had the foresight to wear his old moccasins for this trip, and now he had cause to be grateful. Had he been wearing his boots, chances were they'd have filled with water and dragged him under before he got to land.

With luck, they might even help him outrun those damned pirogues!

Line of the mangrove wall went on around the island, seeming to meet him at every curve of the shore. Anderson swam on doggedly, staying close in its shadow as he felt the strength drain from him. He was almost at the limit of his endurance when the wooded shoreline fell away, giving back to a narrow inlet where the swamp ended in a mass of reed-beds hung over with dark, buzzing clouds of flies. The dark man hauled around and into it, broke stumbling from the water. Rush of slime and water sluiced off him as he staggered upright, the busted hat still dangling from his neck. Shirt, pants and flesh alike were drenched, steaming now under the warm fall of rain. Anderson hit through a stretch of scummed, greenish-black water that reached ankle high, and flung himself into the nearest of the reed-beds. A cluster of birds took flight as he landed, and the dark man watched them circle above him, calling one to another. Anderson burrowed through the first mat of reeds and plunged waist-deep into a pool of marshy water. He floundered on to the second, denser reed-bed, dragging across the mud to slide in between the shielding stems. Anderson lay flat to the ground, easing slowly backward to sink to his hips in reed-fringed mud and water. Parting the stems in front of him, he risked a look.

The running man couldn't have been far behind him when he first reached land. Now he broke from the swamp and stumbled forward, reeling to stay on his feet. Anderson was still trying to figure out who he was when the pirogue loomed out from the slackening rain, nosing around the shoreline to follow the fleeing *hombre* down the inlet. Prow of the boat rammed into the mud as the lurching figure blundered through the first reed-bed, men springing out to come after him with guns in their hands. By the time the running man neared the second bed of reeds, ploughing through the water to his waist, Anderson knew who he was looking at. Aguirre had shucked off his boots and was running barefoot, but the braid on his sodden, mud-splashed uniform was enough to identify him to the hidden man in the reeds. That, and the gash that still wept blood into his eyes. He was halfway across the pool to Anderson when the first shots sounded, the bullets cutting spouts of water from the surface. Aguirre choked, flinging up both arms to fall. He rolled underwater for an instant, and burst clear again, hauling himself painfully to land. Behind him the pursuing bunch came on at a loping run, jogging through the shallow pools towards him as the last of the rain splattered down.

Anderson reached a hand down for the soaked butt of his holstered gun. Swore softly, thinking better of it. The .45 Colt Single Action Army with its 7½ inch barrel had taken a thorough sousing from the time he'd left the boat, and he got the feeling it wasn't about to do him much good. Besides, there looked to be seven or eight men in the group that were chasing Aguirre, and to his way of thinking that was too many for him to be taking on alone without a gun to help him. And from what he'd already seen, Aguirre himself was out of the fight.

He foraged around in the patch of reeds nearest to him, and reached to break off a hollow stem. Anderson eyed the snapped stalk uncertainly, frowning as the noise of pursuit edged closer. This was something he'd never tried himself, but right now it looked like he didn't have much choice. It was either hide out, or be gunned down like a dog.

He only hoped this was about to work.

Scrabbling noises beyond the bank of reeds warned him, and he remembered Aguirre. Anderson stole a swift glance between the stems, in time to see the stricken officer claw his way up the bank towards him. He gained the lip of the reed-bed almost as the dark man peered out, and the two of them met face to face. For an instant Anderson froze, unable to pull away from what he saw. The pale, scared face with its weeping gash above the brow, the mouth that ran blood at the corners. The fixed, uncomprehending stare. Then the ragged volley smashed from further back, the noise of the explosions deafening in the quiet of the reeds. Aguirre gave a hoarse, anguished cry, his body flinching as the shots tore into him. Blood sprayed from his open mouth to spatter the reed stems, and his head flopped sideways into the mud. Anderson watched the captain's hands clutch the reeds in a last frantic spasm before they and the dead man who owned them slid backwards out of sight.

The chasing bunch were a way closer to him now. Already he heard their yells of triumph, the splashing sounds as they fought through the marshy pools. The dark man took a breath as the echoes of the gunshots hit back over the reeds, and spared a glance for the stem he held. If it didn't work, he was already as good as dead.

He fitted his mouth around the hollow stalk, and slid down into the water.

Beneath the surface of the pool the water was as dark and molasses-thick as the swamp had been before. Anderson felt the weight of it press on him as he pushed himself down, crouching on the muddy bed as the scummy surface closed above him. He chose a spot in the shadow of the reeds, one he hoped they'd be less likely to try and fight their way through. Down there, breathing through the hollow reed, he waited. Wasn't nothing else left for it, he figured.

The move he made was none too soon. He'd barely settled underwater when the first of the bunch topped the mudbank, hauling Aguirre's slack body between them. They let the dead man fall in the reeds where Anderson had been lying only moments before.

He heard them come down through the reeds, felt the surge of water that washed against him as they hit through the pool where he lay hidden. Anderson did his best to turn to stone, his breathing the only movement as the group of men plunged by him. Nearest of them passed him by inches, the white of his cotton-clothed leg striking close against Anderson's face. The muddy swirl that followed cut his vision, and he didn't see any more, hearing the muffled sound of voices ebb gradually away to quiet.

He waited out the silence that came after for what felt like a couple of centuries, wary of moving too early and giving himself away. Only when his straining lungs threatened to burst did he let go of the reed and raise his head above the surface of the pool. The stillness of the reed-beds met him, the bunch of bushwhackers gone from sight. Nothing moved along the inlet but the birds that still wheeled in flight overhead. That, and the drone of the hovering flies above the reeds. Anderson didn't move for a while, crouched in the muddy pool and wheezing for breath like a broken-down old man. When he figured it was back to something like normal, and the furious hammering of his heartbeat stopped kicking his ribs like a runaway horse, he eased slowly upright, and hauled his way out of the water.

Last of the rain had passed over, a harsh sun breaking loose to strike the inlet to fire. Fierce light blazed from the surface of the pools, and the marshy ground steamed in the heat. Anderson steamed along with it, his soaked clothes drying out on his body from the ferocious sunlight. The dark man gave a last look at the sprawled body of Aguirre, already overhung with a black cloud of flies, and tipped the water out of his hat. He crammed the bullet-holed thing on his head, pushed the wet hair out of his eyes. Anderson turned his gaze inland beyond the reed-beds to where the ground sloped upward in a green, leafy mass of foliage crowned with a small stand of timber. He shrugged at last, his expression hardening. But the one way for him to go, the dark man decided. Only other chance he had was the mangrove jungle and the swamp, and that was no chance at all.

He headed up the next mudbank, striking his way inland through the beds of reeds.

He was plastered from head to foot with threads of slime and stagnant water that stank to high heaven as it dried and steamed in the heat. Anderson bore with it the best way he could, bore too with the gathering mass of flies that hung and swarmed around him. They settled to bite whenever they could, and after a while he tired of swatting them off him, and let them be. From the feel of it, he reckoned they must all of them have teeth like lobo wolves! His face and body were already itching and swollen from the biting they had taken when he broke out from the reed-beds, and struggled uphill into the thicker brush on the slopes.

He made it to the cover of the nearest clump of bushes, and threw himself down in their shade. By now he figured he was too beat and worn out to take another step, consciousness flickering like a rushlight in a gale as the weariness moved in to claim him. The dark man sighed, face to the ground as his eyes began closing. He'd got himself into one hell of a fix this time, all right. Sure, he was alive, but only just, and there was no telling how long that was about to last. Meantime it looked like Aguirre and the *federales* were all dead or captured, and he reckoned he'd need some luck to get his own gun working again. And so far, not so much as a glimpse of the bastard who was behind all this. The man he'd come here looking to find.

Thoughts swam together, blurring inside his head like mud until they made no sense at all. Numbed to the bone with exhaustion, Anderson relaxed at last, scarcely feeling the dark wave of sleep as it washed him under. One last, half-formed thought came to him before the light went out.

Where the hell was Salazar?

★ ★ ★

Ahead of him an out-thrust branch barred his path, meeting him with a loaded mass of green, fleshy leaves. Salazar reached to hook the bough aside, ducked beneath it to plunge deeper into the overgrown tangle of brush beyond. Behind him he could hear the muffled crash of gunshots, and the hoarse, desperate cries of those who ran and died. Fighting his way through an interlocking mesh of foliage, kicking himself loose from the creepers that hung like thick green ropes from the boughs, the big man cursed, sweating hard in the smothering heat. This expedition had been doomed from the beginning, he told himself. Ever since the two of them had met with Aguirre to agree a strategy, it had been hopeless. The officer of *federales* was a man conscious at all times of his own vanity and self-importance, a man who did not care for outsiders, however good their advice. Now, thanks to his stupidity, their ambitious plans had come to nothing. Thanks to Aguirre an entire

21

unit of federales had been destroyed, and Salazar was running for his life in this accursed jungle somewhere in the heart of Tamaulipas.

Above the trees the rain still came down hard, warm sprays of droplets plummeting through the leaves to churn the narrow trail to a morass of mud. A speckled brown snake darted across the open in front of him, and Salazar froze for an instant, thankful for his heavy boots. To be sure, they left tracks in soft earth such as this, but they had their uses. Thus far, he had been more fortunate than most. His had been the one pirogue to outrun their ambushers, making it around the far side of the island to a stretch of sandy beach free from the mangrove thickets that barred off the land in every other place. There had been three pirogues when they began, but two had overturned during the flight, and the men who lived had been forced to swim ashore. With the boats of their pursuers gaining fast, and picking off luckless stragglers in the water, there had been no time to regroup. Those who survived to gain the beach had scattered like a bunch of panicked hens, each man seeking his own salvation in the dense green jungle beyond.

The trouble with such luck as this was that it could not hold forever. And now the shouts and gunfire at his back told him that it was due to end very soon.

Salazar swore viciously, stretching to drag another low-hanging branch aside. It whipped back to his sudden grasp, and showered him with water from its soaking leaves. The *rurale* captain shoved his way through, biting his teeth hard together as he stumbled on a jutting root and almost went down. About him the jungle dazzled with its glaring wall of green, the boughs with their fleshy leaves glistening and smoking with steam to the humid fall of rain. The heat of the place threatened to overpower him, and Salazar brushed a damp sleeve at the sweat that sheathed his face. This was a misbegotten country, the big man decided. Heat and moisture sucked the juice from a man to leave him no more than an empty husk. To stay here for long would be death to him, even if he managed to get clear of these *ladrones* and their guns.

Where was Anderson now, he wondered.

Hurried thud of booted feet gave warning some distance behind him, and he forgot Anderson for the moment. Salazar dived sideways off the trail, ploughing his way through the bushes that lay closest. Weight of his powerful body sledged into the undergrowth, making a hollow space large enough to admit a man if he bent himself almost double. Salazar hunched into the gap, squatting to draw his knees beneath his chin, and drew the Tranter pistol carefully from the black army-style holster whose buttoned flap hung open. Settling back in the shadow of the foliage, he waited.

24

Two *federales* broke into sight from a clump of bushes further back, both of them plunging headlong up the trail Salazar had followed. The watching captain saw that they still held their rifles, but neither seemed interested in using his weapon, their scared faces and frantic, stumbling haste testimony enough to their fear of what came behind. The first man went by Salazar's hiding-place at a staggering, terror-stricken run, clawing his way uphill through the bushes and the straggling roots. The other had all but reached Salazar when fresh calls sounded close behind him, and more figures burst out from the thickets, guns in their hands. From where the big man crouched in hiding, they showed as little more than greyish outlines against the falling screen of rain.

"Stay put, feller!" It was the nearest of them who shouted.

Sound of it threw the soldier, held him rooted for the moment that counted. He broke from his trance a split-second later, flinging the rifle-butt up to his shoulder in a hurried, instinctive move. He was way too late. The thud of the impacting bullet seemed to reach Salazar almost as the gunflame stabbed from the muzzle. Slam of the shot struck after, and the *federale* pitched back to hit the bole of a nearby tree, the unfired rifle clattering loose as he reeled and went down. The first soldier was gone from sight, only the quivering foliage left to mark his passing. Salazar sat tight in the hollow he had made, watching the three *hombres* who now advanced through the rain and the drifting gunsmoke.

Just the one shot, he thought.

He stayed watching, his thumb curled ready at the Tranter's hammer as the group halted by the fallen soldier, less than a couple of yards from his own hiding-place. From where he crouched in the cover of the leaves, he could hear their voices.

"Looks like you fixed him good, Sharrock." This wasn't the *hombre* who had called out first, but he sounded just as mean. Salazar felt the gruffly-spoken words echo inside his skull, caught the mirthless chuckle. "Near to blowed his haid off, from what I kin see."

"He ain't gonna be no trouble now, I reckon." The voice that answered had a softer, menacing sound to it, and Salazar recognized the man who had fired the shot. Now the gunman was so close, the hidden *rurale* captain could make out the shape of his fancy, hand-tooled boots through the sheltering brush. Salazar heard that voice strike at the others, curt in impatience. "Let's go find the other sonofabitch, okay?"

"Right with you, Lee." The third *hombre's* voice was cowed and quiet. Sounded like he knew who was running the show, and that it wasn't him.

Ducking his head by a shade, Salazar risked a cautious glance through the leaves. The leading gunman was closer than he had thought, so close that Salazar could have reached out and touched him had he felt dumb enough to try it. Fixed as he was, the Mexican stayed hidden. Alone against three killers like these, he knew he was overmatched, and stood little chance of coming out alive. Instead, he studied the *hombre* in front, whose figure now showed clearly against the thinning fall of rain. The gunman was small and slightly built, with cord pants and a fringed buckskin jacket covering him from the wet. Salazar's gaze took in the lithe, narrow-hipped body, guessed at its whipcord hardness. Beneath the wide-brimmed Stetson with its snakeskin band the features too were thin and hard, the eyes black and alert, the flesh pulled taut over high cheek-bones. The skin was also black, a smooth deep shade of ebony that caught the light with a reflected gleam. For an instant the man they called Sharrock turned towards him, his glance raking the thicket where Salazar was hidden. The *rurale* officer endured that questing stare, thankful of the leafy boughs that shielded him from sight. Only when his heart threatened to burst out through his ribcage with its ceaseless pounding did Sharrock turn away at last. Salazar watched as he and the other two struck off the trail and into the quaking foliage, the way the other fleeing soldier had gone.

He stayed where he was until long after the sound of their movement had died away to silence, waiting out what seemed an endless stretch of time as unseen birds chattered overhead, and the lower branches dripped moisture on the back of his neck. It was a while before Salazar eased the last of the sheltering boughs aside, and emerged on to the trail. He stood there a moment in the shadow of the nearest tree, slowly regaining his breath as the thud of his heart grew calmer and less hurried. A tall, broad-shouldered figure of a man in his leather shirt and cords, the felt *Chihuahueno* shading his face. Salazar's features were broad and Indian-dark, with a splayed nose and thick-lipped mouth, the knife-scar showing livid against the thick black stubble that coated his jaw. A brutal face at first glance, the kind of face that belonged to a *bandido* or a hired killer. It told but half the story of the man behind it. Salazar drew a long, unsteady breath, the right hand holding the Tranter pistol lowered to his side. He turned back the way he had come, aiming to cut off from the trail further down and maybe shake off anyone else who followed.

The dead soldier still lay sprawled in the wet earth at the base of the tree. The captain of *rurales* halted for a moment in passing, looked down into the other's upturned face. The bullet-hole made a neat black circle between the staring eyes, back of the ruined skull mercifully hidden from sight. Salazar eyed that hole and swallowed hard, his grasp of the pistol tightening. This Sharrock *hombre* was one in a thousand, the Mexican decided. No one else he knew could have made a head shot from that distance, and with such speed. He would do well to keep out of the way of this one, if he could.

He had straightened up from the body of the *federale*, and was set to move on, when the sound of another voice froze him in his tracks.

"No foolish moves, Salazar," the voice said.

It came from deeper into the bushes on the right of the trail, and the sound of it was enough to tell him he had no chance. Salazar bit down on a curse and waited, holding the gun low to his side. Left side of the trail, further back, he saw the branches shake, and knew he had more than one to deal with. Back of him, the voice from the right spoke again.

"Throw down the gun, *hombre*. We have no time for games."

Salazar pitched the weapon from him, scowling as he heard it strike the dirt. He turned, both hands raised now, to meet the man who stepped from cover. The gaunt, tall figure in the white *peon* garb, so tall he overtopped Salazar by a head. The man who now held the sawn-down shotgun by its pistol grip to bring both 12-gauge barrels level with his gut.

"This is indeed fortunate, Salazar," Amarillo said. "I had hoped to find you here."

He came out on to the trail, halting maybe a couple of yards away from the *rurale* captain with his shotgun still lined on the other's belly. Seen in the open, he seemed to gain in height, rearing spectrally tall against the sparse boles of the trees. Salazar took in the worn serape that hung from one shoulder, the bandolier with its three throwing knives. From deep in the shadow of the straw sombrero, the face with its lean, harsh features broke into a mocking smile. "That is much better." Amarillo's face had a bronzed, yellowish hue to it, the features so gaunt as to be almost skeletal. Salazar met the stare of those deep-set amber eyes, and felt the touch of ice along his spine. He knew the hate that this one stored, the way a rattler harboured its venom, and didn't need to be told what he had in mind for old enemies such as himself. He watched as the gaunt man gestured with a jerk of the head, and other figures stepped on to the trail from either side, their own guns levelled. Salazar stayed rooted to the spot, both hands lifted. Not a hope in hell, he thought.

"Two questions, Salazar." Amarillo still smiled. His voice, though, held the same chill menace. "Who sent you here, and where is Anderson?"

Planted helpless in the middle of the trail as the others closed in around him, the *rurale* captain forced himself to meet that yellow-eyed stare. For the moment at least, he disregarded the shotgun muzzles that threatened his belly. It was not the way of Amarillo to kill quickly. Whatever it was he devised for Salazar would be slow and painful, as it would also be for Anderson.

"It is for you to find out who sent

us," the Mexican said. He fought the unwelcome quiver in his voice as he spoke. "As for the other matter, if I knew where he was, I would not tell you, be sure."

He stood, hearing the silence that came after the words as it rang like thunder in his ears. About him the faces of his captors showed hard and merciless, ready to spring on him and cut him to pieces at a word. Only the gaunt face of Amarillo kept to its smile, the yellow-eyed half-breed lowering the shotgun he held so that its muzzles no longer pointed at Salazar. Instead he cradled the weapon easily in the grip of both hands, stepping closer, his smiling features inches from Salazar's own face as he spoke again.

"In time, you will tell me where he is," Amarillo said. "Until then, we are done with talking."

He moved swiftly in the same instant, whipping the shotgun upwards in a tight, vicious arc. Salazar sensed the blow coming and tried to bring down his arms against it, but the movement of the taller man was too quick. Butt of the weapon thudded on his jaw, and the ground went out from under him. Falling, he caught a momentary glimpse of the arched green foliage above him, then the darkness flooded his senses. He did not feel the impact of the wet earth as he struck.

The last thought that formed in his mind in falling brought him no comfort. It seemed to Salazar that they had run their heads into a noose, and Amarillo held the rope.

Maybe, this time, they would not win through, after all.

2

BARK of the gator warned him a couple of seconds before it showed. The sound came from the thick foliage that lay fifteen to twenty feet ahead, and carried to him plain enough to stop him in his tracks. Anderson stayed put and kept his distance as the massive reptile broke cover, crossing the narrow trail at a quick, scuttling run. Monstrous critter, all right, anything up to twenty feet from nose to tail. It swung its head sidelong as it went, the stare of the eyes above the broad wedge snout coming to rest on Anderson, standing further back down the trail. The dark man sucked in his breath, hand faltering towards the useless gun at his side, but this time he was in luck. The gator spared him but a glance, and figured he didn't count for much. Anderson stayed watching as the huge, armoured shape launched itself across the track and into the brush on the far side, sunlight gleaming on its greyish treebark scales as it slid downslope for the water. Answering barks came from the reed-fringed pool away to his left, and the tall *hombre* swallowed, easing his tongue around leather-dry lips. Gators didn't rate too high on his list of likes, but he'd never doubted that they were smart. Maybe this last beauty had him figured pretty good, at that. Alone, and with nothing better than a knife, he had to admit that he didn't pose much of a threat — to gators, or anything else.

Then again, he was still standing and breathing while most of the others were dead. And that had to be a start, at least.

Anderson scowled, shook himself out of the last of his trance. He struck forward along the trail that took him deeper into the dense growth of jungle ahead, quickening his pace to a steady lope. Sooner he was out and above the gator-pools, the better he'd feel.

He followed the narrowing track as it moved upslope, burying itself in the jungle that carpeted the higher reaches of the island in a vivid explosion of green.

Nightfall found him on higher ground, camped in shelter of the trees that rimmed a clearing. Lightning had made the notch in the jungle timber, blasting a live-oak taller than the rest, that had fallen to smash a corridor of its own through the surrounding foliage. The trunk of the dead giant spanned the clearing, its outline hung thick with creepers and pale fungoid growths that gathered to hide both bark and leaves from sight. Anderson eyed the felled mass from a distance, settled on his heels in the deeper shadow of the trees. The fire he'd built an hour or so back was burning well, and the swamp rabbit he'd managed to snare on his way here was roasting on its makeshift spit above the flames. Scent of the cooking meat teased his nostrils, but the dark man left his meal untended for the moment, his glance shifting to where the .45 Single Action Army lay in pieces on his open bandanna, spread on the dead oak's weathered stump in company with the gunbelt and its shells. Anderson crossed over to the weapon and studied it for a while. Nodded at last, satisfied. He'd dried out the Colt and cleaned it the best way he knew how, checked on the powder and percussion caps in the .45 shells. He figured he'd need to oil the gun and test it out a little before he could be sure, but right now it was as close to working order as he could make it. He gathered the parts and fitted them together carefully, set the weapon back into its holster. Anderson slid the bullets into their leather loops, and buckled the gunbelt around his waist. He moved back to the edge of the clearing and settled down, drawing his long-bladed knife from its sheath. Salt water hadn't done it too much good, but the blade still cut cleanly through roasting rabbit haunch. Anderson sheared the leg from the animal on the spit, tore hungrily at the succulent flesh. After a day without food, it tasted better than ever. He hoisted the carcass off the spit, and kept right on eating until there was nothing left but the bones.

Night deepened over the island, darkness flooding the clearing and the surrounding jungle in a black, impenetrable tide. Noise echoed through the trees as it came, raucous, piercing calls of birds that Anderson had never heard in his life before. Stealthy, furtive slithers of movement came through the thick undergrowth at the clearing's edge, and far into the distance, the fainter sound of gators barking in the reed-beds. Anderson shivered, peering vainly against the mass of darkness all around him. He killed the fire and lay down, digging himself in by the roots of the trees with their carpet of moss and creeping growths. His hand lay on the knife-haft as he slept.

He was back in Las Cuernas, and it was daylight, the harsh sun beating into his eyes through the window cut high in the adobe wall. Anderson ducked his head, squinting against the unbearable dazzle of light. Across the room, he could hear Romero's voice.

"You have been brought here for a good reason, *señores*," the man from Mexico City was saying. "Our government faces difficulties in Tamaulipas, which may not be easily overcome by conventional methods. Our information is that men and weapons are being shipped in large numbers from Galveston and other ports in Texas to the Tamaulipas coast, and that a base is being established there with the intention of moving further inland and occupying the sovereign territory of Mexico." The pause that followed seemed to last for several minutes, as if allowing time for the shock of its message to sink in. Then, abruptly, Romero spoke again. "The name of the *Americano* behind this invasion is unknown to us at present, but there can be no doubt that his aim is to seize a part of our country by force, and impose his will upon it."

"You are talking of men and weapons, Señor Romero." That was Salazar, from away to Anderson's right. His eyes still half-closed, the dark man smiled as he heard that hard, deep-chested voice cut across the room to where Romero sat back of his battered desk, his figure framed upright against the adobe wall. "What kind of men are they, and what guns do they carry?"

"They are killers, Señor Salazar." Romero spoke patiently, as if addressing a difficult child. "Soldiers of fortune, gunfighters, the name does not matter. What counts is that murder is their trade, and they are many. The word from Tamaulipas is that we have at least fifty *gringos* to deal with, and that they are well armed with revolvers and repeating rifles. Worse, they have allies on this side of the border, which may serve to swell their numbers further."

He halted for a moment, and in the brief silence Anderson could feel the force of those dark eyes fixed upon him across the room. "That is why you are here today, *señores.*"

"How come you reckon we're gonna take care of business?" sound of his own voice came back to him strangely, as though heard from a remote distance. "Ain't no way the two of us kin deal with more'n fifty gunsels, an' that's a fact!"

"You will not be alone, Señor Anderson." Romero had begun to sound impatient, his tone clipped and hard. "A unit of *federales* has been assigned to accompany you on this mission, a total of sixty men in all. At the moment they are camped less than a day's journey from here, at Nuevo Fronteras. These men will be at your disposal, my friends. Their commander has already been instructed to co-operate with you, and to be guided by your suggestions before any course of action is taken."

"So why us?" Anderson wanted to know.

"Two reasons." Voice of the government man had lost none of its icy sting, cutting at him like a whiplash from the far side of the room. "Firstly, this region of Tamaulipas holds problems for any straightforward military operation. It is a country of lakes and mangrove swamps, of thick jungles and saltmarshes infested with unpleasant reptiles. Such a region would appear to be more suited to the talents of *guerrilleros* like yourself and Salazar, who are known to excel in country where a simple soldier would be lost."

"If that's the way you see it." Anderson sounded less than convinced. From beside him, Salazar butted in again.

"The second reason, Señor Romero, if you please." The *rurale* captain's voice rang harshly, its echoes hitting back from the closed corners of the room. When the man from Mexico

44

City answered, the ice was gone from his tone, only a sombre chill remaining.

"We do not know the *Americano* who brings in his gunmen from the north," Romero told them. "The name of the man who is their ally in Tamaulipas, however, is known to us." He paused, the sound of his voice grown weary as he spoke again. "This one has troubled us many times before. He is known to you also, *señores*."

"Amarillo, right?" Anderson breathed the words tightly, through his teeth.

"As you say, Amarillo." Romero sighed, rustling the papers on his desk. Anderson heard the rickety chair scrape backward as the official pushed it closer to the wall, its unsafe legs protesting at the move. "My friends, you are the only hope we have in this matter. You alone have fought this *serpiente* and bested him, not once, but several times. No one else could be trusted to hunt him down, and bring him the justice he deserves. Amarillo is too cunning, too dangerous, for us to leave him in any other hands but yours."

"Maybe not even ours." Anderson's voice was grim. The dark man frowned in thought, still ducking his head to the light from the window. "Could be the sonofabitch will be too slippery for us to take a grip. Wouldn't be the first time he's got by us, an' that's the truth."

"Better that you should not let this happen," Romero told him. "If you fail us in this matter, Señor Anderson, then we are lost. In such an inhospitable region, Amarillo and his American friends will be able to build up their defences, until not even an army will drive them out. *Quien sabe?* Maybe, in time, Tamaulipas will not be enough for them, and they will try to seize even more of our country . . . "

"Okay, okay. I get the picture," Anderson breathed out fiercely, shaking his head. The tall man straightened in his seat, one arm lifted against the sunlight that speared into his eyes. "Seems to me we got no choice but to take the job on, like it or not. Right, Mig?"

"*Verdad, amigo.*" The voice of the *rurale* captain carried the same weary resignation. Eyes narrowed to the glare, Anderson glimpsed the broad, stubbled features of the Mexican, caught the other's forced smile. "Two of us against Amarillo this time, Andres. Maybe together we shall be too much for him, eh?"

"I'll sure as hell drink to that," Anderson said.

Sound of his voice seemed to echo, reverberating strangely as the words were spoken. All at once the sun-blasted room blurred and swam from sight, and he was no longer at Las Cuernas. Instead he and Salazar were stepping ashore from the boat that was moored at the rickety landing stage, the two of them walking up the slope of a sandy beach to where a group of uniformed *federales* stood waiting. Sun seared his back like molten metal, struck hard as a fist between his shoulders. Anderson endured it without a word, striding on with the hot sand scorching the soles of his mocassins. Beyond the uniformed shapes he made out the huddle of log-walled, sod-roofed shacks with the flag of Mexico flying above them, that he figured must be Nuevo Fronteras.

One man stood forward of the group, he noticed. Tall, slender *hombre* whose uniform looked to be overgrown with medals and gold braid, his shoulders weighted down by heavy epaulettes. Seemed to Anderson he could feel this one's stare fixed on him as the pair of them gained the crest of the slope. He and Salazar reached the waiting bunch, and came to a halt, studying the face of the man before them.

"Andrew Anderson," the dark man said. "This here's Miguel Salazar of the Sonora *rurales*." He grinned then, leaning forward to extend his hand to the waiting officer. You'll be Aguirre, I reckon."

Face of the uniformed *hombre* gave no answering smile, stayed hard and closed as he looked the two of them over. He kept his gloved hands low by his sides, fingers aligned with the seams of his flared riding-breeches, making no attempt to take the other's offered hand. Anderson met the keen, deep-set gaze of those jet-black eyes as they studied him from beneath the peaked cap with its badge of eagle and serpent, and read no hint of friendship there.

"You are addressing Captain Ramon Pascual Aguirre y Ibarra, officer of *federales* and servant of the government of Mexico." Sound of the voice struck at him viciously, at one with the merciless glitter of the eyes. Aguirre drew himself to his full height, his cold stare measuring the taller man from head to foot, and back again. "In future, *hombre*, you will speak when I give you permission to do so. What is more, you will salute me as your superior when you speak to me again. Is this understood, Señor Anderson?"

Harshness of the words froze the grin on Anderson's lips, halted the extended arm with its offered handshake. The dark man bit down on a sudden surge of anger that threatened to overwhelm him, both fists clenched at his sides as he fought to hold himself back. From close beside him, Salazar spoke.

"We are here on the instructions of Señor Romero, adviser to the President in Mexico City." Voice of the *rurale* captain came hard and stubborn in answer, tight as a drawstring as it struggled to contain its anger. "It was his word to us that we are to advise you, and that you are instructed to co-operate with us. Your unit is to be placed at our disposal, captain. Furthermore, as civilians, we are not obliged to obey military commands . . . "

"You are here under my orders, Señor Salazar!" Aguirre cut him short, leaning closer to glare up into the face of the big *rurale*. The hard, narrow features of the captain whitened along their cheek-bones, a thick vein pulsing at his temple as he all but choked on the words. "I am aware of my instructions, and need no advice from such as yourself on how to carry them out. It is for me to decide what will be done here, *hombre*! Not yourself, and not this *gringo* friend, this *pistolero* you have brought with you to Nuevo Fronteras. Until such time as our mission is accomplished, you will do as I tell you, and obey orders with the other men of my command. Is this understood, *Capitan Salazar*?"

He laid emphasis on the *rurale's* rank, making no effort to hide the sneer in his voice. Watching, Anderson saw the other's broad face darken, tautening in fury, and wondered for a moment if his friend was about to take a swing at the bemedalled dandy in front of them. Instead, Salazar mastered his rage with a visible struggle, composing himself to speak once more.

"Señor Romero told us . . . " he began. This time, though, he got no further.

"It is not Señor Romero who

commands here, *hombre*!" Aguirre all but screamed the words, his face inches from that of the *rurale* captain. "Here I am the one who leads, and it is my orders, and only mine, that are to be obeyed! As captain of *federales*, I outrank yourself and your friend, Salazar, and you are therefore placed under my command. Do you understand this, *hombre*?"

Salazar said nothing for an instant, his stubbled face defiant still as he glanced sidelong at Anderson. The dark man met that glance and shook his head, shrugging his shoulders resignedly. Right now, he didn't trust himself to speak. Back of their commanding officer, the unit of *federales* stood uneasily to attention, sweating in the fierce heat. Anderson studied the impassive faces of the young, boyish lieutenant, a couple of hard-bitten veteran sergeants, the smooth *Indio* features of the troopers further beyond. No help there, he figured. All of them were acting under orders. Now it looked like he and Salazar were too.

"It is understood, *capitan*," Salazar said. He sounded like the words were about to choke him. Eyeing him levelly, Aguirre nodded, beginning for the first time to smile. All things considered, Anderson figured he'd as soon have the officer as he had been before.

"*Bien. Muy bien.*" Aguirre turned his unpleasant smile Anderson's way. "And what of yourself, Señor Anderson?"

Right now, I'd take pleasure in busting your jaw, the dark man thought. For once, though, he kept the thought to himself.

"Understood, captain." Seemed like he could taste the slime on his answer, and it didn't agree with him at all. Anderson grimaced, swallowing on defeat. In front of him the officer of *federales* smiled more broadly, his bared grin matching the row of sunlit medals on his chest.

"Much better, Señor Anderson," Aguirre nodded, his voice losing some of its hardness. Beneath the peak of the decorated cap, though, his dark eyes stayed cold. "You are learning now, I think." Abruptly, he turned on the bunch of troopers behind him. "Company, dismiss!"

Anderson watched as the kid lieutenant and the sergeants barked the order like echoes, and the group of *federales* broke apart, scattering away towards the log buildings beyond. Aguirre paid them no attention, turning back to where the other two men still stood waiting.

"Your kind are not new to me, *señores*," the captain told them. By now, he was no longer smiling, his narrow features hard and closed as they had been before. "I have worked with *guerrilleros*, and I know their ways. It is in your nature to be undisciplined, and to act without authority. On this mission, such initiative will not be permitted. I will decide what is to be done, and you will follow my orders to the letter. There is no more to be said, *hombres*."

He paused, the tight smile threatening once more under his pencil-thin moustache, and pointed to the largest of the log-walled shacks behind him.

"Come with me, my friends," Aguirre said. "Now that we understand each other, I will tell you how this task of ours is to be accomplished."

He turned, striding stiff and straight-backed across the hot sand towards his quarters. Anderson watched him go, feeling the heat of the sun as it punished his head and shoulders. He was thinking of the three thousand miles that he and Salazar had come to arrive at this place. The endless, risky desert journeys aboard ancient locomotives that threatened to blow their boilers at every uphill grade. The muleback and horseback mountain crossings through the foothills of the Sierra Madre. The briefing at Las Cuernas, and the trip downriver to Nuevo Fronteras. The pair of them had put their lives in danger a hundred times in Yaqui and bandit country just to get here. And now that they'd arrived, it looked like it was all going to be for nothing.

He glanced across to Salazar, read the same anger in the Mexican's face. Anderson swore, hitting a fisted hand against his thigh. He went forward, the *rurale* captain beside him as he followed that strutting figure towards the buildings of Nuevo Fronteras.

Drowsing half-awake, the dark man sighed, recalling the way it had gone. Aguirre had been the worst kind of fool, Anderson decided, a man whose own self-importance came before everything else. Thanks to that sonofabitch and his vain stupidity, he and Salazar had been given no chance to do the job they'd been hired for. The *federale* captain had refused their offer to go in and scout the islands under cover of darkness, had scarcely allowed them out of his sight. The sixty-strong unit had moved downriver in open daylight, and launched its attack across the swamp by pirogue in the middle of a rainstorm,

Aguirre sticking rigidly to the times he had set, and making no allowance for adverse weather. Amarillo and his American friends must have seen them coming hours before the attack, and had all the time they needed to set up the ambush that had cut the *federales* to pieces. Remembering the hail of fire from the islands, the falling bodies and the overturning pirogues, Anderson groaned, shifting uncomfortably against the tough tree-roots. What should have been a surprise attack had proved to be no better than suicide, the unit all but wiped out with hardly any losses suffered on the other side. And all of it down to Aguirre, damn him to hell!

Memory came to him of the stumbling, mud-smirched figure in the reed-beds, the gashed brow and the fixed sightless stare of the eyes. Anderson breathed out slowly, the worst of his anger fading as he moved half-asleep at the base of the tree. Aguirre had paid for his mistakes the hard way, the dark man reminded himself. No way the captain of *federales* could be brought back to answer for it now.

Only pity of it was, that he'd taken so many with him!

He woke, eyes opening sudden on the darkness about him. Silence answered, thick enveloping quiet that pushed down heavily on him until it almost seemed he had trouble breathing. Anderson lay motionless in the shadow of the tree-roots, his flinty gaze searching the leafy crowns that arched to a mass of dark overhead. The call of a nightbird shivered from the distance, and someplace further out he could hear the slithering movement of one of the smaller critters as it went hunting in the darkness, but it wasn't for them the dark man listened. So far neither sound nor movement had come to warn him, but he didn't need them to know. Whatever it was that had brought him awake, it was still here with him. Anderson felt the presence in the throbbing of his sharpened senses, the stiffening of the back hairs on his neck. Scouting against the Apache taught a man to trust that kind of feeling, especially when it helped him stay alive.

Cedarwood butt of the Colt lay under his hand, already halfway clear of its holster. Anderson rolled slowly sideways, eased the weapon free in a gradual, unhurried move. He lay by the dark base of the tree-bole, ears straining for the smallest sound as his eyes probed the night and his thumb edged itself over the hammer of the gun.

Silence grew tighter around him, caught him like a noose at the neck. Anderson lay still as stone, waiting for the tell-tale sound. When it came it was no more than a faint whisper of movement, but the unnatural quiet set it ringing in his ears like a gunshot, impossible to miss. The dark man let it come to him, tracked it to a point at the edge of the clearing maybe a dozen yards from where he lay. His pale eyes intent on the spot, he lined the Colt and waited.

Fresh shift of movement broke the night gloom between the boles, outline of a lone figure showing darker on the darkness. Anderson watched as the shape edged forward to the rim of the clearing, halting for an instant as if unsure whether to come on or turn back into the trees. Anderson eased the muzzle of the big Colt sideways, until the foresight cut the shadowy outline apart at the waist. He slid up on to his haunches, weight poised lithely on the balls of his feet as he came fully upright in the shadow of the trunk nearest to him, his gun still levelled on that figure at the clearing's edge.

"Come ahead or die, *hombre*," Anderson said.

He spoke softly from his hiding-place by the tree-bole, taking care to make no sudden moves. Across the clearing he saw the dark shape freeze to the shock of his words, grown in a moment to a motionless pillar against the background of jungle foliage. Anderson gathered his breath carefully, keeping the Colt in line.

"*Quien es, hombre?*" the dark man said. Then, more fiercely, "Come forward, or I will fire."

"*No tiran, señor*," the voice said.

The figure came ahead in the same instant the words were spoken, stepping warily into the open with both hands lifted. Anderson said nothing for awhile, shocked in turn by what he heard and saw. Closer in, the shadowed outline took on a more definite form, of a kind that could not be mistaken. It confirmed what the sound of that voice had already told him — that this was no man he held at gunpoint, but a woman.

"I am called Juana," the voice told him. Listening, he caught its low, husky sound, heard too the hint of fear that trembled behind the words.

"Come ahead, Juana," Anderson said. He didn't lower the gun.

Inwardly, he still had trouble coping

with what he'd heard. A woman, here in this godforsaken jungle. Fixed as he was, Anderson figured he already had the odds stacked against him. Chances of his getting clear of the islands and the swamp were slim enough, let alone any hope of bringing in Amarillo and the rest. Now it looked like he had a lost woman on his hands.

He sighed then, feeling the weariness creep back into his bones. Sure was one hell of a note, he thought.

He lowered the gun slowly so that the muzzle pointed to the ground, and waited for her to come to him.

3

"WHERE is he?" Amarillo said.

Held fast by other hands in the chair at the centre of the room, Salazar made no answer, defiance plain in the set of his harsh, stubbled face. Above him, stooping against the low roof of the cabin, the gaunt man sighed.

"Give me his hand," Amarillo said.

He spoke to the six men beyond him. The bunch of dark-featured Mexicans in the white *peon* clothes that matched his own. The ones he called his angels, who now clustered around the figure in the chair. Pack of them had Salazar pinned before the sentence was finished, two men forcing his arm rigid and the fingers of his hand open as the *rurale* captain struggled vainly to free himself. Amarillo felt the spatter of moisture strike his nape from the sod roof overhead, and dismissed it from his mind; ignored, too, the hissing rush of rain outside. He stepped in closer, his hard yellow eyes fixed on the face of the man in front of him.

"This time you will learn manners, Salazar," the gaunt *hombre* told him.

He took a grip on the thick, ragged fingernail with the steel tongs he held, and hauled backward with all his strength. Salazar yelled like a wounded beast as the nail cracked, ripping its way out from the flesh. Amarillo studied the agonized face of his prisoner, and smiled. He heaved back in a second, wrenching lunge, and the nail came away in the grip of the steel jaws, leaving the bloody flesh behind. For a time the only sound was the moaning of the man in the chair as he fought against the pain.

"Sweet Jesus God," Lee Sharrock said.

He stood back of the gaunt man in the shadows of the room, his hand laid over the holstered pistol-butt as if seeking reassurance from the familiar smooth feel of the hardwood grips. Sharrock heard the anguished yell of the Mex and felt it tear through him, caught the sickening sound of the nail wrenching loose, the drip of blood to the beaten earth floor. The slender gunman grimaced, swallowed down on a surge of bile in his throat.

Amarillo heard the other man call out behind him, turned his gaunt head halfway around towards the sound of that voice. Sharrock locked stares with the tall half-breed for an instant, forcing himself to meet the gaze of those merciless amber eyes. Amarillo's narrow Indian face betrayed nothing of what he thought, his features stony and expressionless as he looked the other man over.

"Maybe you should not stay to see this, my friend," Amarillo said.

Sharrock didn't answer, disgust showing plain in his look. The gaunt man eyed him for a few seconds longer and shrugged, turning away again. Amarillo bent close above Salazar, who hunched in the chair, shuddering visibly as he fought the onset of nausea together with the pain. This time the half-breed did not smile.

"You would be wise to tell me what you know," the gaunt *hombre* said. Then, in a harder, insistent tone: "Where is Anderson?"

Salazar brought up his head with an effort, gasped against the pain that shot fire through his mauled finger-end. His face was ghost-white and sheathed in sweat, and he couldn't see for the water in his eyes. It was a while before he could speak at all.

"I do not know where he is," the big *rurale* answered hoarsely through fresh, sickening waves of pain. "And if I did . . . "

"*Bastante!*" voice of Amarillo broke in on him, hacked away the last of his words. The gaunt man gestured impatiently to the waiting 'angels', who crowded in again, stretching the bloodied arm forward. "You have not learned obedience, *hombre*. It is a hard lesson, and in your case it must be given more than once. The hand, *compañeros*!"

He closed in, the tongs already showing a dark stain at their jaws as he made to take a fresh hold. Behind him Lee Sharrock puckered his lips on a sour taste, and spat for the far corner of the room.

"Damn if I aim to stick around for more of this," the gunhawk said. Sharrock started for the doorway that showed itself as a dim outline in the shadowed gloom ahead, flat of his hand still resting on the pistol-butt as he went. His voice struck at Amarillo as he crossed the room, cutting harder than a blacksnake whip. "You sure as hell somethin', feller, you know that? God knows, I seen men die before now — killed more'n a few myself, in my time — but I ain't never seen nothin' to match this before. Mister, you got to be the sickest son of a bitch I set eyes on in my whole goddamn life!"

He lunged past the taller man as the words were spoken, quickening stride as he made for the door. He'd all but reached it, when the voice of Amarillo stayed him.

"*Un momento*, Sharrock!" the gaunt man called.

Sharrock felt the impact of the other's voice strike him, sensed the venom that lay behind the words. He halted, turning slowly back around to face the bunch in the darkened room. Amarillo had swung away from the huddled figure of Salazar. Now he loomed tall as a spectre against the low roof, the lean-fleshed face drawn taut on its bones as those eyes raked Sharrock like chips of yellow stone.

"You called me an evil name, *hombre*," the half-breed told him. In the sudden quiet that filled the room, his voice rang unnaturally loud. "Among my people, that is a killing matter."

Sharrock heard the menace in the

other man's words, and for an instant felt a chill travel like icewater down his spine. Then the moment passed, and his own self-possession returned, the cold, controlled man-killing mood that had served him so well and so often before.

"Could be I did," the black gunman said. He smiled, a mirthless grin that matched the deceptively gentle sound of his voice. "You want to make somethin' of it, maybe?"

His small, long-fingered hand slid over the butt of the .44 Remington Army in the moment he spoke, thumb easing on to the weapon's hammer as his fingers settled on the grips. Back in the middle of the room he saw Amarillo stiffen, one hand lifted to the bandolier of knives that crossed his chest. Beyond him, the six 'angels' had begun to reach into their belts for sheathed pistols and machetes, their eyes on Amarillo as they waited for the word. Sharrock stayed planted firm, legs straddled as he dropped into his half-crouched gunhawk's pose, his upper body leaning forward. For the space of several heartbeats his eyes and Amarillo's locked together, the silence stretching out between them until it threatened to tear apart.

"Another time, perhaps," Amarillo said. He moved his hand slowly from the haft of the topmost knife, the yellow stare hard and cold in his stony face. The gaunt man signed to the group behind him, who shifted hands from their weapons. His look, though, stayed with the gunman in the doorway. "This time you have been lucky, my friend. Do not expect to be so fortunate again. *Sabe usted*?"

"Any time you care to name, I'll be waitin'," Sharrock said.

He turned his back on the half-breed, pushing out through the open doorway to the bucketing rain. Behind him he heard Amarillo call out harshly to the other men in the room. Sharrock grimaced, guessing what was about to come next. He bit down on the vile taste in his mouth, easing his hand away from the gun as he ducked outside.

He heard the hard, drumming sound of the rain that hammered the makeshift verandah above his head, felt the spattering fall of water that struck through leaves and gaps in the wood slats to hit warmly on his neck and the backs of his hands. Bradley Gill shrugged off the random droplets, shook briefly at the arms of the yellow oilskin slicker that gleamed in the wet. The thickset man let the cigar burn down a notch where he held it between his stubby fingers, his gaze shifting outward to the country ahead. Beyond the cleared compound and its sod-roofed cabins, the lie of the land broke away in a gradual downhill sprawl, green riot of jungle yielding to the darker mass of mangrove swamp as it dipped to merge with the water. Masked as it was by the downpour and a hanging mist, Gill reckoned he couldn't mistake it. Nothing but rain

71

and swamp and jungle as far as the eye could reach. That's all there was from here to Matamoros and the coast. Gill peered into the hissing curtain of rain that screened the jungle further back, falling to churn the compound to a morass of thick, gluey mud. Misbegotten country this, whichever way you looked at it, he thought. Maybe he wouldn't have come here, if he'd known.

Warmth of the cigar between his fingers reminded him. The stocky man shook off the momentary doubt with the drops of rain from his slicker, shifted the cigar-stub adroitly to the corner of his mouth. Gill smoked a while in silence, his moustached features frowning in thought as he watched the heavy downpour speckle the brown pools in the compound. He'd have been a damn fool not to come here, the thickset man told himself. The chance that he was being offered in this neck of the woods was way too good to be missed. Fact that it was a godforsaken hole where it never quit raining for more than a half-hour at a time made no difference at all.

Above the storm-lashed compound the cloud-mass wrenched itself apart, a faint light breaking through to fall on the figure by the wall. Limned by that momentary shaft of light, Gill frowned again, drawing on the last of his cigar. He was a burly thickset man in a yellow oilskin slicker, his short legs out of proportion with the powerful upper body and massive hands. A wide-brimmed J. B. Stetson shaded features that were heavy and smooth but for the greying moustache that overhung the upper lip and gave him something of a walrus look, his close-cut hair stippled with grey at the temples. Gill's eyes were grey too, pale and cold as seawater in the ruddy, cleanshaven face. They matched the thin hook of nose and the small mouth that gripped the cigar as if to pinch the life from it. Gill smoked it down to a useless butt and pitched it from him, frowning still as he watched it strike the nearest of the puddles in the open ground.

Back inside the cabin came sounds of movement, and a man's voice bellowing in sudden pain. Bradley Gill heard that cry, more like a wild beast than a man's in its fearful agony, and shrugged, putting it from his mind. Man got nowhere unless he was prepared to get tough with the difficult customers, the stocky *hombre* told himself. Amarillo knew it, and so did he, and that was why the two of them made a good partnership. Neither one of them was in it for the good of anybody but himself, and that meant that both would do their damnedest to make sure it worked. And if any lawjohn, Mex or otherwise, decided to get in the way, then so much the worse for him.

He breathed out the last cigar smoke, smiling a little now behind the thick moustache as the faint whorls drifted off into the rain. Up to now things had run pretty much to schedule, Gill reflected.

Thanks to Amarillo and his greaser friends they'd managed to establish themselves here on the island, and wiping out the immediate opposition had been far easier than he'd expected. Dumb sons of bitches had walked into the ambush with their eyes shut, and the whole thing had turned into a turkey-shoot. With nobody left to stand up to them for the next couple of months, and the handful of surviving *federales* all but hunted to a finish, he figured there was little enough for him to worry about. In the next two or three days the reinforcements should be arriving with their shipment of arms and supplies, and once they were dug in the place would be secure. From there, it would be but a short step to move on the provincial capital, and in time extend operations beyond Tamaulipas itself.

He drew himself up to his full stocky height, shoulders braced firm as he savoured the aftertaste of the cigar. Gill thrust both hands in the side pockets of his slicker that he'd had custom-made back in St Louis, smiled a little tighter as he thought of the way it had been. Hell of a distance from here to Wyoming, and the First International Bank of Stockmen and Commercial Trades that he'd set up in Cheyenne with a couple of partners more gullible than himself. He'd already worked out that there was more money to be made in illicit deals than in banking, and was the place's biggest customer in an unofficial way — from the day it opened for business. Gill had robbed his own bank blind, drawing out thousands of dollars in the guise of loans for a group of associates who acted as front men for the enterprise, whose claims were underwritten by Gill himself. Working in this underhand fashion, he'd managed to siphon off almost two hundred thousand before the deal turned sour. Bitter, freezing winters of the late 80s had wiped out entire herds to put the local ranchers out of business, and the disaster forced a run on the bank. Once the loans were called in, there was no way the fraud could be kept a secret. Gill and his friends had barely made it out of town ahead of the lynch mob, and over the ensuing days the law had run most of them down. Bradley Gill had managed to get aboard the first train south. What was more, he'd made sure that the money travelled with him.

Union Pacific brought him to St Louis, where he'd set to work on his latest venture. Money talked there the way it did everywhere else he'd been, and Gill made certain it was used to his advantage. Word had got around in the right quarters of a job in Old Mexico, and of the high wages that were being paid. Pretty soon, Gill had all the seasoned gunhands that he wanted, together with the promise of enough ammunition and supplies to back an army of invasion. From there the action had moved to Galveston, and some hard bargaining with the local shipmasters. What Gill had in mind was against the law, and that being so the price came higher, but he was well placed to meet it, and the deal had gone through without a hitch.

Behind him in the cabin the silence broke apart to a second scream of pain. Gill listened to the harsh, animal sound, barely registering an interest as it wavered and died away. Amarillo had proved a valuable ally to them here, the thickset *hombre* told himself. Gill's contacts had put him in touch with the half-breed before he came to Galveston, and the deal had been struck between them by the time the shipping arrangements were settled. It was thanks to Amarillo that the enterprise had succeeded so well and so quickly. He'd handled the Mexican side of the business, scouting out the swamp islands as a useful base for operations, setting up temporary quarters here, ensuring that the landings went ahead safely. His hired men knew the creeks and thickets of this territory like they knew their own names, and they had friends in the larger settlements inland.

It had been their word that had alerted Gill and his army to the arrival of the *federales*, and Amarillo had helped them lay the ambush that put paid to their attack. No doubt about it, the breed had been worth his own weight in gold. If he got his kicks from torturing some greaser captain half to death, so what? Gill didn't aim to lose any sleep over a little thing like that.

He nodded then, still standing square in the shelter of the porch, a hard, determined look replacing the smile on his moustached face. Up north they still had him figured for a charlatan, a fraudster who had cut and run once the going got tough. Tamaulipas offered him the biggest chance he was likely to get, the chance to show the world that he ranked with the great leaders of the century, the men of destiny whose eminence set them beyond morality and the rule of law. With the money and men at his disposal, he would conquer and rule Tamaulipas, might even go on to become Emperor of Mexico itself! Gill set his jaw stubbornly, thrusting out his chest to match the image in his mind. Wasn't as dumb as it sounded, no sir! After all, they'd had an Emperor in this country not much more than twenty years back. Look at what Napoleon had achieved in Europe, at the start of this century. And Garibaldi, too — he'd captured the whole of Sicily with only a thousand men, back in 1860. Who was to say that Bradley Gill couldn't do the same, here in Mexico? Hell, he even had the look of them, didn't he? That Napoleon had only been a little guy, and from what he'd heard of Garibaldi, he wasn't so tall either.

He stared ahead into the downpour that hammered the compound, the thin smile returning slowly. By God, that was the truth of it. A man of destiny, no less. And this was the place where he'd prove it to them all!

He was still standing there, hands in the pockets of his slicker and that cold smile on his face, when footsteps thudded in the doorway behind him and Lee Sharrock ducked outside to join him.

"Come on out, Lee," Gill kept to the smile, not troubling to turn his head. "Make yourself at home." Peering forward into the fiercely hissing rain, the thickset man chuckled softly, a chill sound that matched the steel-grey glint of his eyes. "Impressive, the amount of water this place soaks up, isn't it? Ship it over to Arizona or the Staked Plains, we'd be rich as kings."

A couple of paces back of him, the black gunman didn't answer, his narrow features taut and frowning from what he'd already seen. Gill felt the silence strike at him and frowned in turn, allowing his glance to shift sidelong until the figure of Sharrock registered at the corner of his eye.

"Something bothering you, Lee?" the stocky man asked.

For a moment, the gunhawk stayed quiet, right hand gripping hard on the butt of his leathered .44. Back into the cabin the Mexican prisoner had begun to groan in a faint, hoarse voice that sounded close to unconsciousness. Above that sound, the two of them heard Amarillo's sudden, ringing laughter.

"That's one sick bastard you got back there, Mister Gill," Sharrock said. There was no way of mistaking how he felt, revulsion drawing his voice so tight that it all but shook as he spoke. "I seen better mad dogs in my time, I reckon."

He broke off, breathing hard, and brushed both palms down the front of his worn cord pants, as if to rid himself of something he'd picked up on the way outside. Ahead of him, Bradley Gill's small mouth hardened impatiently beneath the heavy moustache, his hands clenching to fists in the slicker pockets.

"Not getting a touch sentimental, are we, Lee?" his own voice bit at the man behind him. Hearing it, Sharrock shook his head, anger still tightening the muscles of his face.

"You know that ain't never been my way, Mister Gill," the gunman muttered.

"Glad to hear it," Gill's voice didn't soften at all, eyes grey and hard as gunmetal beneath their shaggy brows. The businessman still made no move to turn around, hands out of sight in the oilskin coat as he held the lean-framed *hombre* at the rim of his vision. "Fact of the matter is, Lee, I hired you to do a job, same goes for all the men on my payroll. You remember that, and we'll get along just fine. Understand?"

"Way I see it, you got no call to rebuke me, Mister Gill," Sharrock said. Though his voice came soft, it held a steely menace of its own. Sound of it brought the head of Bradley Gill around, and for an instant his pebble-grey stare met the black, stony gaze of the gunman behind him. "Up to now I done everythin' you paid me for, an' I reckon you'd travel a ways 'fore you found yourself the man could do it better! Ain't that the truth, now?"

"Maybe you're right, at that." *Hombre* in the slicker still frowned, aware of those dark fierce eyes scouring him from head to foot. He never looks away from you, Gill thought. Never see him look down or off to the side. Always meets you head-on, the way no nigra should have a right to do. Times, it could be a mite unsettling. Aloud, he said: "It's Amarillo I'm talking about this minute, and you know it. He works for me the same way you do, Lee. Long as I pay the wages, you leave him be. All right?"

Up by the wall of the cabin, Lee Sharrock sighed, his lithe narrow body hunched as he shook spatters of moisture from the shoulders of his buckskin shirt. The black gunhawk reached into his breast pocket for tobacco sack and papers, his thin ebony features harder than stone as he rolled himself a smoke. "That sonofabitch don't work for you, Mister Gill," Sharrock said at last. He spoke softly, almost inaudibly, around the cigarette he held wedged in the corner of his mouth, his black eyes measuring the stocky man ahead. "Paid or not, he's the kind always works for hisself an' nobody else. Should it suit his convenience, he'd sell us out with no more trouble'n it takes for a grain-fed hoss to blow off his wind. What's more, I reckon you know it."

He struck a match on the heel of his boot, touched the flame to the cigarette. Above the sudden flare of light his dark gaze held level, gleaming hard in the lean midnight face. Gill met that stare and felt his fists bunch tighter in their pockets, last of his temper running out like a foot of sputtering fuse.

"What he does is none of your concern, you hear?" Anger caught his voice, gave it a higher, shrill edge that he hadn't intended it to carry. Gill's thickset body stiffened beneath its oilskin covering, his teeth gritting together as he glared into the other's insolent eyes. No way Napoleon would have stood for that kind of answer, he told himself, and what was good for him went double for Bradley Gill. "You draw my wages, Lee, you take my orders and like 'em! Right now I'm giving you an order. Amarillo is my business, and you leave him lie. Got that?"

"I hear you, Mister Gill." Lee Sharrock shook out the guttering matchflame, threw the stub from him into the nearest puddle. The thin, slight figure drew easily on his cigarette, hard gaze still on the businessman as he breathed out the smoke. "That's the way you want it, you got it, I reckon. Just don't expect me to cotton to him none, is all."

"Never said anything about your feelings, Lee." Gill's voice thawed by a touch, but not so much that you'd notice. "Long as you keep them to yourself, I'll be happy." Abruptly, his broad face cracked its harshness, a tobacco-stained smile baring itself through the walrus moustache. "Let's put this little difference behind us, okay? No reason why we shouldn't be able to disagree and still be friends."

"Whatever you say, Mister Gill." Sharrock drew the cigarette from the corner of his mouth, lips curling back in a lopsided grin that revealed his own white, strong teeth. Meeting that smile, Gill decided that nobody else he had ever known could put so much sarcasm into a smile, or make an apology sound so much like an insult. "Already done forgot the whole thing, count on it."

"That's good. Very good," Gill smiled affably in return, unclenching his hands in their oilskin pockets. "Matter of fact, the news gets better all the time, Lee. Word from our scouts is that we need expect no further military intervention before the year end, and several of the landowners in the region appear to be disaffected with the provincial government, and ready to throw in with us. By this time next year we'll be out of these damned swamps, and pushing for the capital." He let the smile broaden through the hairy mass of moustache, pebble-cold eyes studying the man by the wall. "What do you think of that, my friend?"

"Sure sounds fine to me, boss." The black gunman had the smoke back in the corner of his mouth, speaking tightly around it. To Gill's ears, he didn't seem overexcited by what he'd been told. Now his eyes fixed on the stocky hombre like slivers of gleaming jet, holding chill and level above the flaring tip of his *cigarilio*. "Ain't found us nothin' yet that me an' the other fellers cain't handle, Mister Gill. An' once that there shipment comes through from the coast, I reckon we should have it well sewn up between us. Ain't that so?"

"You bet it is," Bradley Gill's ruddy face beamed amiably, the smile breaking wide beneath the thick moustache. Somehow, though, none of the warmth from it reached those pale, seawater eyes. He brought a beef hand free of his slicker, leaned to clap the other man on a buckskin-clad shoulder. "Stick with me, Lee, and you'll be set for life. Better believe it."

"You pay good, Mister Gill, an' that's the truth," Sharrock told him.

"Only for the best." The heavy-set man in the slicker chuckled, patting the thin, whipcord muscles of the shoulder through its buckskin coating. Gill figured he'd won now, and could afford to be magnanimous. "Every man I've hired has earned his corn, and you're the pick of the bunch, Lee. I've yet to see the man that could match you with a pistol, either side of the border. Even Wes Hardin would find you a handful, I think."

"Hardin ducked me one time," Sharrock said. Remembering, his lean ebony face went closed and hard behind the cigarette. "Don't talk of it overmuch, from what I heard."

"Just why did you come out here

with me, Lee?" For once, Gill's voice was curious.

"Tole you before, you pay good." The gunman frowned, shrugging his narrow shoulders. Back of the smoke, his hard eyes gave nothing away.

"That ain't all of it." Gill wasn't satisfied, his own gaze questioning the man at the wall. "Something more than that, I can tell. Seems to me you have other reasons for being here in Tamaulipas, isn't that right?"

"Maybe so." Sharrock's dark face stayed closed and impassive. The gunhawk smoked his cigarette down, and trod it underfoot, eyes with Gill as he ground the butt under his heel. "Somethin' you kin tell me, Mister Gill. Just who in hell is this Anderson feller I been hearin' about?"

"Some two-bit lawjohn, I guess. Runs a *pueblo* up in Sonora." Bradley Gill spoke curtly, dismissing the problem before it arose. "I gather he and Amarillo have had a few brushes with each other in the past. Nothing more than that."

"Seems like friend Amarillo come off second best, don't it?" Sharrock's narrow-lipped mouth cracked to the thinnest of smiles, the eyes bright stones in the smooth ebony of his face. "Judgin' by the way he's treatin' that other poor son back there, he cain't wait to get a hold of this Anderson *hombre*, which ain't the way no man behaves when he's won the play before." He paused, the tight smile hardening as his look turned thoughtful, calling some other thing to mind. After a while the gunman nodded. "Come to think, Mister Gill, I reckon I might just've heard of the guy, at that. Apache Anderson — yeah, that's the one, all right!" He glanced across to the thickset man, who now stood staring ahead to the rainswept compound. "Figures hisself as some kinda gunfighter, ain't that right?"

"I really wouldn't know about that." Gill glowered at the relentless downpour in front of him, squaring his broad shoulders as if to shut off the other's question. "Let's face it, the place is crawling with men who think they can handle a gun, same goes both sides of the border. You're different, Lee. Not a man of them could match you if he tried."

"Yeah." Sharrock had regained his tight, narrow-lipped smile. "Guess you right enough there, Mister Gill."

He was still thinking about that when Gill called out to him, grabbing at his arm with one hand as he used the other to point into the rain. Following the line of that out-thrust finger, Sharrock caught sight of the stumbling shape that broke from the far side of the compound, heading towards them. Figure of a man hunched low against the sheeting fall of rain, lurching and staggering to stand as he fought his way through the pools and the slick, treacherous mud. He went down a couple of times, splashing headlong in one of the largest puddles in the compound, and clawed back to his feet plastered with mud and water. Gill and Sharrock made no move to help him, stayed watching as he made it to the cabin, and dragged himself into the shelter of the leaking porch. The *hombre* slumped against the wall, struggling to get his breath. He was one of Amarillo's Mexican gunhands, sent out with others to scout the island a few hours before. Now he eyed the two Americans uncertainly, his black sloe eyes wary and untrusting in the broad Indian face.

"Señor Gill!" He spoke the words hurriedly, still gasping for breath as he shook himself like a dog, his drenched clothes spraying water. Thick red mud coated the white cotton rig with its shellbelt bandoliers, the straw sombrero and threadbare serape. Moisture dripped from the lank black hair, wept from the moustaches that overhung his mouth. "Señor Gill, we have found others . . . "

"What in hell you talkin' 'bout,

feller?" Lee Sharrock asked.

Sound of his voice hit before Bradley Gill could open his mouth, cutting at the *hombre* by the wall. Hearing, the Mexican hesitated, his glance switching from Gill to the man beside him. The dark *Indio* eyes fixed on Sharrock with a cautious, grudging respect. He had seen the way the black one handled a gun, and knew better than to make him angry.

"A *pueblo, señores.*" The gunman forced himself to speak more slowly, taking care over his words. All the time he spoke his eyes shifted rapidly from one to the other of the listening men. "On the far side of the island, *señores* — a village, in the woods. There are *peones* there, with their women and children."

He halted, breath sawing hard in the momentary silence as he fought to recover himself. Bradley Gill frowned as that silence fell, his pebble-grey stare turning hard on the *hombre* by the wall.

"That's something we hadn't counted on," the businessman said. He gripped one hand tight to his side, closing the fingers, as if crushing a bothersome fly. "Sooner we clear it up, the better, I'd say."

He let his glance shift across to where Sharrock stood beyond him, the grey stare coming to rest on the buckskin-clad gunman as the words were spoken. The thin-featured man read that look in a moment. Nodded coldly, not speaking.

"*Señores*," the Mexican spoke again from his place by the wall, eager to be gone, "*Señores*, if you will permit me . . . I must speak to Señor Amarillo . . . "

Gill didn't turn back to him, nodding abruptly in dismissal as he gestured towards the open door. He and the black gunhawk were still trading sombre glances as the man plunged from sight into the room beyond.

Inside the cabin, Mig Salazar groaned and slumped over in the rickety

95

chair, his head falling forward on his sweatstained chest. Watching him, Amarillo shrugged, losing his amused smile for a moment. The gaunt half-breed nudged the pliers halfway open, letting the third ripped nail drop to the floor, and wiped the bloody jaws on the leg of his cotton pants.

"*Bastante, hombres*," Amarillo said. "When he wakes, we will begin again."

He signed to the waiting angels, who released their hold on the unconscious man, stepping back to the darker shadows in the corners of the room. Amarillo had moved to lay the pliers on the table behind him, and was cleaning his stained hands on his breeches when the sound of voices outside alerted him, and the rainsoaked figure stumbled in through the doorway behind.

"*Que pasa*, Jesus?" Amarillo demanded.

He stood, stooping a little beneath the low overhang of the cabin roof, his hard yellow eyes on the man before him. Jesus cut loose in answer with a torrent of Spanish, and the gaunt man let him tell it, breaking in now and again with further questions. Around him he could sense the gradual build-up of tension in the room as the listening angels heard what the other man told him. After a while, Jesus slowed for breath again, and Amarillo nodded, lifting a hand to cut him short.

"You have told us enough, Jesus," the half-breed said. In the gloom of the cabin his hard yellow eyes gleamed, cold and pale against the darkness. "*Gracias, amigo*. This was well done, be sure."

"*Por nada, mi jefe*." Jesus ducked his head, smiling in relief. For a moment he had feared that the tall man would blame him for what had been found. He had seen others who suffered the anger of Amarillo, and it was not a good thing to look upon, still less to endure. "It was the task you gave me, nothing more."

"As you say, Jesus." Amarillo appeared to have dismissed the drenched scout from his mind, already turning away to hoist his weapons from the table. The gaunt man slung the bandolier of throwing-knives from his shoulder, hefted the sawn-down shotgun with its smooth pistol grip. As he tugged the wide-brimmed straw *sombrero* to cover his head, those amber eyes scanned the waiting faces of the men around him. "*Adelante, compañeros!* There is more work for us in this place than we thought."

He picked out a couple of his angels from the rest, and left them to keep watch on the unconscious figure of Salazar. Amarillo turned and made for the open doorway, the bunch of hard-bitten Mexicans following him. The faint sound of his rope *guaraches* vied for an instant with the hissing downpour outside as he reached the opening and ducked, stooping to go through. Ahead of him he could see the sombre, anxious faces of the two Americans, and knew that they had also heard the message of

Jesus. Stepping into the open to meet them, Amarillo smiled, tightening his grip on the lowered shotgun he held.

Maybe Anderson would be there too, he thought.

Out beyond the verandah, the hard rain hammered the compound, mud and puddles steaming as the drumming of the downpour shut out all other sound.

4

"NOW you see me, *señor*," the woman said.

She stepped into the centre of the clearing, and stood there, looking to him with both hands held low by her sides. What light there was came in through the gap the deadfall had made, and struck full upon her, showing her to the man who waited in the deeper shadows. Anderson didn't answer for a moment, the long-barrelled .45 lowered as he studied the figure in the open ground. The figure of a tall woman with a powerful, heavy-set build, the mass of coarse black hair hiding her face like a horse's mane. From here, he could see that she held no weapons in her hands.

"I see you, Juana," the dark man told her. This time his voice came a touch gentler than before. "Now tell me what you are doing in this place?"

Something in what he said sparked her anger, caused her body to stiffen as the hands clenched at her sides. Juana shook back the mane of hair, and bared her face to him. It was an Indian face, Anderson saw, smooth and broad-featured, the cheek-bones high and heavy and the eyes black and gleaming as polished shards of jet.

"This is my home, *señor*," Juana said. She made no attempt to hide the defiance in her voice. "I have always lived in this place. It is you who are the stranger here."

Anderson heard the anger that lay behind her words, read the fierce spark in the depths of those eyes, and smiled for the first time.

"True, Juana," the dark man said. He shrugged, the smile turning rueful. "I am called Andres. I came to the island with the *federales*, but they were waiting for us when we arrived. Many of my *compañeros* died, but I was lucky, and escaped with my life . . . "

"I was there, Andres," Juana said. "I saw what they did. They are animals, all of them."

Her broad face clouded at the memory, anger and disgust mingling together in her look. Anderson said nothing, his own glance still taking in the woman before him. He saw that she was dressed in the loose white blouse and full, patterned skirts worn by most Mexican *peon* women, with her arms and legs bare, and her feet unshod. Anderson eyed those powerful, muscular arms, guessed at the tough, calloused skin on the soles of the feet. No wilting society female, this, but a strong, weather-hardened woman used to heavy work on the land. Strong-minded, too, from what he'd already heard. Not to be easily scared by a stranger with a gun in his hand. He stayed quiet as he watched, waiting for her to speak again.

"It was a month ago they came here," Juana told him. "We saw them from a far distance, but did not show ourselves. We have learned it is not wise to tell strangers that we are here on the island, unless we have looked them over first." She paused for a moment, her broad features frowning as she called that time to mind. "Many pirogues, Andres. Many men. All of them with long guns and *pistolas*."

"How many men?" Anderson wanted to know.

"*Quien sabe?*" The woman shrugged, spread her big, blunt-fingered hands. "Forty men, perhaps fifty."

"*Mejicanos?*" The dark man eyed her carefully as he spoke.

"Some of them," Juana nodded, meeting his gaze levelly. "Most of them, though, are *gringos*. Three men lead them, who are worse than the rest. One man, in *peon* clothes, very tall, who carries an *escopeta* . . . "

"Amarillo." Anderson's lean face showed grimmer than before. "Him I know from way back. We have been enemies for many years."

"He is the worst of them," the

103

woman said. "The other two are *Americanos* — one is a white man, short, *un poco gordo*." She outlined the pot-bellied shape with her hands. "The other is not so fat, *un pistolero negro*. He has already killed many."

"A black gunman, huh?" This was something Anderson hadn't been expecting. Her dark eyes on his, Juana nodded again.

"*Verdad*, Andres. I have seen him."

"*Gracias*, Juana," the dark man said. His own look still questioned. "What did these *hombres* do, when they came here?"

"To us, nothing. They did not find us." Juana found time for the faintest of smiles. "Our village is well hidden, on the other side of the island, and so far they have not discovered us." She halted, the smile fading slowly from her lips. "They settled on the near side, where the land faces into the great swamp, the way you came. They built *casas* and *jacoles* for themselves there, to shelter from the rain, and cut down trees to clear the ground around them. Some days they would send out scouts to search the jungles, but we were careful, and they found nothing. We had only to look at them, to know they were *malo hombres*."

"Then we came to the island," Anderson said.

"As you say, Andres." She studied his harsh face warily as she answered. "You came, and the bad ones were waiting. Our people knew that something very bad was to happen . . . I went out with the others to see . . . "

"Hell of a thing to watch!" The dark man's voice was fierce, thick with anger. "Wasn't nothin' but a massacre. We had no chance!" Seeing how she stood with her calm, stolid gaze fixed on him, he shook his head, last of the rage leaving him in a heavy sigh. "So what happened to you an' the others, after?"

"The storm separated me from them," Juana told him. For the first time a tired note entered her voice, as though even the telling wearied her. "When the rain grew less, I was far from the village, and the bad ones were in the marshes all around, hunting down the *federales* who lived. I hid in the jungle until the night came, and made my way back to join my people." She paused, eyeing him thoughtfully from where she stood in the open ground. "That is when I saw you, Andres. I have followed you here, to this place."

"The hell you say!" Catching the glint of amusement in those eyes, Anderson grinned wryly, shaking his head. "Looks like you had time to look this stranger over anyhow, Juana. You figure I can be trusted?"

"I trust you, Andres," the woman said. Now she smiled openly, taking a step in closer from the middle of the clearing. "We saw that you came with the *federales*, and how the bad ones would have killed you. You are their enemy, and that makes you the friend of our people. *Sabe Usted?*"

"I reckon," Anderson nodded, feeling

the tension ease from his body. The dark man moved to sheathe the unfired pistol, smiling in answer. "So, here we are, Juana. What happens now?"

"We go to my people." At once her voice grew firm, more sure of itself than it had been. Juana held out her hand to him, drawing him after her as she started back towards the clearing. "Come, Andres! With me you will be safe, they will not find you!"

She set off at a striding pace that was somewhere between lope and run, dragging him behind her as she followed the shadow of the felled tree spanning the open ground. The strength of her woman's hand surprised him, the blunt fingers closing to imprison his own in a firm, unbreakable grip. Anderson made no move to fight it, plunging after her as best he could. By now it had dawned on him that he was the lost one around here, and that Juana was doing the rescuing. Anderson had owed his life to a woman before, but it wasn't something that happened too often. While the thought of it this minute struck him as kind of unusual, he figured he could learn to live with it.

Way he saw it, it was a whole lot better than being dead.

They reached the far side of the clearing, skirting the massive, outspread roots of the deadfall, and gained the deeper shelter of the trees beyond. Once they were into cover, Juana released her hold on him, slowing to walking pace as she went on ahead. The dark man followed, cat-footed in his moccasins, leaving space between the two of them but making sure he kept her in sight. He could scout and track with the best, and his half-Indian senses were keen, but in the dark and in this unfamiliar country he was more than happy to let Juana lead the way. Now he stalked along the path she made for him, ducking the hanging mass of creepers to follow a series of narrow, overgrown trails that he reckoned he'd have had trouble finding in daylight, eyes fixed on the moving shadow-shape in front.

Movement whispered in the over-hanging boughs, and the calls of the night-birds wavered through the tree crowns above him. Away into the swamps, he figured he could still hear the gators barking one to another. Anderson grimaced, picking his way forward over the slippery, littered jungle floor. He kept going, holding Juana in sight as she moved lithe and sure-footed through the space between the trees, following still as the narrow tracks widened to broader lanes and corridors and other small clearings, and the darkness of the night ebbed slowly backward.

It was almost dawn, a grey half-light leaking in through the tree crowns to bleach the dark boles and shrink the shadows to faint puddles on either side of the trail, when the moving figure came to a halt before him. Anderson watched as Juana stepped off the track, hunting the shelter of the nearest jungle trees, and turned, looking back to where he waited. The Mexican woman signed to him impatiently, beckoning him forward, and he broke to his earlier loping run, darting aside from the trail just before he reached her hiding-place. Anderson ducked into tree-shade behind her, his body pressed tight to the closest of the tall trunks that hung shaggy with fungus and slimy growths. A few feet ahead of him, her own palms braced against the bole of another tree that shielded her from sight of anyone further along the trail, Juana met his look, and smiled.

"This is the village, Andres," the woman told him. "We are home now."

She turned from him with the words, edging around the thick trunk to peer at what lay beyond. From his own vantage point, that enabled him to see past her, Anderson did the same. A short distance further on, the trail turned a corner, fading out as the trees gave back to show a huge clearing in the heart of the jungle. Remnants of old stumps, overgrown with moss, dotted its outer rim, and light flooded the open space as dawn began to break through to eastward. The dark man stayed motionless in cover of the tree-trunk, pale eyes searching the ground ahead. A tumbled sprawl of shacks and cabins met his look, makeshift dwellings of logs and deadfall limbs, chinked with swamp mud and roofed with sods and dried palm fronds. Anderson saw a shallow creek that wound its way by the foot of the uphill slope where the buildings clustered, made out the squatting figures of peasant women who beat sodden garments on the stones at the water's edge. Further up the slope, into the jumble of cabins and jacals, he could see windbreak *ramadas*, and heavy, weighted nets that hung stretched and drying on their sapling frames. Reek of smoked fish drifted from the curing sheds that topped the crest, mingling with the acrid scent of morning cookfires. White-clad shapes moved in the gaps between the ramshackle buildings, stooping out from *jacal* doorways to squint against the light. Already some of them were making their way downslope, their faces shadowed by huge straw *sombreros*, the occasional gaunt-ribbed dog barking alongside as they descended the muddy track that led to the creek. Up ahead Juana turned again to him and smiled, weariness and relief mingled together in her look. The Mexican woman eased slowly clear of the shadowing tree-bole, and moved back towards the trail.

Instinct warned him, brought him fully alert before he heard a sound. Anderson felt the tell-tale shiver along his nape, and pressed deeper into cover, reaching down easily to bring the gun from leather. Same instant he made the move he caught the eye of the woman in front, and shook his head. Juana read the message in those harsh, tautening features, frowned uncertainly for a moment. Seeing him lower his hand for the gun, she stepped back from the empty trail, edging cautiously for the dark shade of the trees.

First sound that offered was no more than a whisper, faintest slither of movement in the foliage away to the right. Watching, Anderson saw the quiver of a low-hung bough, weight of an oncoming body that reached to thrust it aside. The figure of a man ducked through the underbrush on the far side of the trail, maybe twenty yards or so into the trees, heading for the clearing. A gaunt man, unusually tall in his white *peon* garb, the straw *sombrero* shading a fierce, hollow-cheeked face. He held the sawn-down shotgun out before him by its pistol grip, the belt with its throwing-knives hung at his shoulder. The tall shape halted for a moment, turned briefly to look their way. Even at this distance, and in cover of the massive trunk, Anderson seemed to feel the impact of those merciless amber eyes. The dark man drew in a breath and held it, forcing himself to stillness. His heartbeat had begun to thud uncomfortably on his ribs when the tall figure turned away unseeing, and slid on through the dense jungle foliage beyond.

"Amarillo!" Anderson let the word come from him low-voiced, an almost soundless release of breath. The worst of the tension left him as he shaped the name, his heartbeat steadying slowly. Looking to Juana, he saw that she had made it to cover in the trees, and now stared helplessly in his direction. The dark man glimpsed the shocked, frozen expression of her face, frowned grimly in his turn. Now he heard other shifting movements in the brush where Amarillo had been a moment before, caught sight of more stealthy figures who edged warily through the shielding boughs and fronds towards the clearing. These *hombres*, too, were garbed in *peon* white, but unlike the men in the village they hefted pistols and carbines, and had the look of killers who had used such things before. Anderson watched from cover, stony-faced. If they were Amarillo's hired guns, they'd have had plenty of practice, he thought.

Beyond them, in the clearing that held the village, one of the running dogs halted and began a frantic barking as it scented the men in the thickets. Other dogs gave tongue in answer, the clamour echoing through the trees. Watching, Anderson saw the *peons* on the track freeze to the sudden racket, caught the shocked faces of the women by the stream as they looked towards the outlying jungle. Almost as they made the move the foliage shook, and Amarillo and his white-clad followers broke cover at the clearing's edge, their weapons levelled on the men and women in the open.

"*Buenos dias, señores — señoras,*" the gaunt man said. He smiled viciously, right hand hefting the sawn 12-gauge by its pistol grip. "You will oblige me by staying where you are. *Sabe Usted?*"

From the far side of the clearing came a fresh surge of movement, and another group of armed gunsels emerged from the cover of the thickets. There were

115

maybe twenty or thirty of them in all, and from here they had the look of Americans, wearing work shirts and cords or denims rather than the white cotton of the angels. In that first momentary glimpse he had of them, Anderson picked out a handful from the bunch that he figured as its leaders. The tall grey *hombre* in the double-breasted shirt, who toted a pistol in either hand. The short, barrel-chested man with the flattened nose, and the gleam of steel *conchos* on his vest. Thin, leather-faced jasper in the derby hat, and a black-bearded bear of a man rigged in plaid shirt and brass-riveted levis, whose right hand clasped a massive .44 Colt Dragoon. Most of all, his gaze fixed on the black, thin-featured *hombre* in the buckskin jacket, who now stepped into the clearing ahead of the rest.

"You heard him, folks!" Lee Sharrock called. The black gunman stood, lining the Remington ahead of him as his sharp-eyed stare raked the open ground and the terrified huddle of villagers beyond. "Just stay right where you at, ain't no harm comin' to you . . . "

Down by the creek one of the women screamed, and the dogs set off to bark again. The sound seemed to break the *peons* from their trance, men and women running to hunt cover among the huts or making for the jungle as others raised their hands, sullen-faced in defeat. Amarillo lined on a stumbling *peon* who turned to head back upslope, and pulled on the trigger. Blast of the 12-gauge charge took the running man full in the back, slamming him to earth. Amarillo used the butt of the weapon to smash the skull of a snarling dog that launched itself for his throat. Around him, and away across the clearing, shots crashed in a deafening barrage as the villagers ran and fell, unable to escape the pitiless guns.

"God damn it to hell," Anderson said.

He saw the white-clad figures blunder in panic-stricken flight, scattering in all directions as the bullets cut them down. Anderson caught sight of a fleeing woman seized by one of Amarillo's bunch, heard her shrill cry of terror as the *hombre* threw her to the ground. The dark man bit down on another curse, feeling the grip of his hand clench tighter on the unfired gun he held. Right now, he couldn't bring himself to look Juana in the eye.

One man against more than thirty, he stood no chance at all. Amarillo and his *gringo* pals were going to do just what the hell they liked here, and there wasn't a damn thing he could do but watch it happen.

All the same, he couldn't help but feel sickened and angry at what he saw.

Inside the clearing, the gunfire stilled abruptly, echoes of the shots dying away through the trees. An unreal silence fell, broken only by the wails of women and children, the whining of dogs, and the noise of men coughing in the reek of gunsmoke that drifted across the open ground. Those villagers who lived stood like stone pillars, their hands in the air as the killers moved forward, picking their way through a scatter of white-clad bodies in the mud. Amarillo was first to them, grasping an old *peon* by his shirt-neck to drag him closer. The gaunt man hoisted the shotgun barrel until its muzzle rested under the *hombre's* chin, wedging itself against the scrubby white furze of beard. Scanning those terrified features, Amarillo smiled again, more cruelly than before.

"You will help me now, *viejo*," the tall half-breed told him. He tightened his grip on the *peon's* shirt, pressing the shotgun muzzle hard against the grizzled jaw. "A friend of ours is lost, we are looking for him. Maybe you can tell us where he is. *Entiende?*"

"*No sabe, señor.*" The oldster barely choked the words, his eyes wide in fear as he read the message in those hard, pitiless features.

"A tall man, in *gringo* dress, but with

119

the face of an *Indio*." Amarillo seemed not to have heard the other man, smiling still as he held him against the gun. "His eyes are grey, very pale for such a face. He is called Anderson, and we know he hides somewhere on this island. There are not many places for him to stay hidden, and this is one. I think perhaps you should tell us where to find him, *viejo*."

"*Señor*, I do not know this man . . . " Voice of the oldster shook, tears welling in his faded eyes as he answered. "There is nothing I am able to tell you . . . "

Meeting those scared eyes, Amarillo lost his smile. The gaunt man paused, his glance cutting over the other villagers whose fearful looks fixed on him. The half-breed sighed, his own stare murderous as it came back again to the man he held.

"That is unfortunate, my friend," Amarillo said.

Crouched in the cover of the trees, Anderson heard Juana's horrified gasp, felt his own body tense at what was coming. Amarillo had already eased the shotgun trigger halfway back when the sound of another voice halted him.

"Goddamit, that's enough!" It was the black gunman who shouted, from the other side of the clearing.

He came forward into pistol range as the words were spoken, his smoking gun held out at arm's length in front of him. Black muzzle of the pistol came to rest on Amarillo at a point between the eyes. Catching the move, both the gunmen and white-garbed angels froze to stillness, eyeing each other uncertainly.

"Turn him loose, Amarillo," Sharrock said. "He don't know nothin'."

He moved in closer, overstepping the body of a *peon* who sprawled face down in the red mud of the clearing with both hands gripping the dirt, the big .44 Remington Army holding level on the gaunt figure ahead. Staring back into that black, unforgiving gun muzzle, Amarillo felt an uncomfortable itching sensation at the point between his eyes where the gunsight rested. He had seen the black one shoot before from this distance, and knew that Sharrock would not miss. Knew, too, that he would not hesitate to fire. The tall half-breed breathed out slowly, easing his grip on the *peon's* shirt.

"This is a bad mistake you are making here, Sharrock," Amarillo said.

He withdrew the shotgun barrel from beneath the *viejo's* jaw, shoved the man fiercely from him. The oldster staggered, sprawling on hands and knees in the muddy earth. He shot a frightened glance backward over his shoulder as he scrambled upright, moving clear of that gaunt figure and the threat of the sawn-down shotgun. Amarillo ignored him, his yellow-eyed stare staying with Sharrock as the buckskin-jacketed gunman halted maybe ten feet away from him, the pistol in his hand still lined on the half-breed's head.

"You risk your life, *negro*," Amarillo

said. Hard as he tried, he couldn't quite hide the anger that thickened his voice. "This is the second time I have warned . . . "

"You aim to do somethin' about it, go right ahead." Sharrock bit out the words, his ebony features drawn taut on their bones. Black eyes of the gunman glittered, cold and merciless as shards of rock. "Ain't gonna git yourself a better chance, an' that's the truth!" His glance shifted from the gaunt man, touching momentarily on the angel who had the woman down, and was busy tearing at her clothes. "Git 'way from her, mister, an' leave her be. This ain't why we're here, an' you know it!"

Down on the ground, the white-garbed Mexican paused, looking up into the other's face. Reading the murderous expression there, he got up slowly and backed away, the woman hurrying to rearrange her disordered clothing as she, too, struggled to her feet. Beyond them, facing the levelled pistol, the tall figure shrugged, lowering the shotgun to his side.

"Another time, my friend," Amarillo said.

Sound of sandalled feet in the mud alerted him, and he swung round towards it, the weapon lifted afresh as his cold eyes sought a target. He was in time to catch sight of the three *peons* who ran headlong to find cover in the thickets that fringed the clearing between Sharrock's bunch and his own. Their sudden, unexpected rush took both men by surprise, the Mexicans almost into the sheltering foliage as the first shots cracked after them. Last man in the group staggered, but stayed on his feet to follow the others, all three making it to cover as the noise of the gunshots died away. Eyeing the heavy-leafed boughs that shook closed behind them, Amarillo swore, his shotgun unfired. The gaunt man turned back to face Sharrock, his harsh features more savage than before.

"Let 'em run, fellers!" the black

gunhawk called out to his own men, some of whom were already starting forward after the fleeing Mexicans. Sharrock met the half-breed's look and shook his head, puckering his lips in the wryest of smiles. "One's hit bad, an' there ain't noplace the others kin go from here! Ain't that right, Amarillo?"

"If you say so, *gringo*." Amarillo's eyes stayed bleak and cold. The tall man studied the cowed group of villagers who bunched together in the middle of the clearing. Took in the scared, beaten faces of the *viejo* and his fellows, the sobbing of the woman who now stood, pulling her torn clothes about her, the wails of young children hiding their faces in the skirts of their mothers. "I think I could still persuade them to tell me where Anderson is hidden, if you gave me time . . . "

"He ain't here, feller," Sharrock told him. The American brought down his gun-arm slowly, easing the muzzle away from Amarillo's forehead as

125

he called again to the men at his back. "Turk! Jimmy! Take some of the boys an' search these goddamn huts, if he's here you oughta find him easy enough. Wade an' Fletch kin stay with me."

Watching from his vantage point beyond the clearing, Anderson saw the *hombre* in the derby hat break from the group, heading a well-armed search party for the makeshift dwellings further up the slope. Behind him the blond, heavy-chested gunman frowned, hesitating as he looked towards Sharrock uncertainly.

"You gonna be all right back here, Lee?" the short man asked, and Sharrock nodded, dark eyes still on Amarillo as he smiled.

"Sure, Turk. I kin handle it," the man in the buckskins told him. "Git along now, you hear?"

"Anythin' you say, feller." Turk Laban shrugged, moving awkwardly through the mud to catch up with the rest. Meantime, at the head of the bunch backing Sharrock, the black-bearded gunsel scowled, his narrowed gaze hungry on the huddled mob of *peons* by the creek.

"No reason why we should pass up on the women, I reckon." Sound of his voice came deep and heavy, rumbling in the massive chest. "Seems to me we earned ourselves a little fun, an' they ain't nothin' but a pack of greaser bitches anyhow . . . "

"You tellin' me I don't give the orders here, Fletch?" Sharrock didn't bother to turn his head, but his voice cut like a lash. Hearing, the bearded giant scowled darker, looking down. "You do like I tell you, feller. Same goes for all of you gunnies behind me. We ain't here to slaughter oldsters an' kids, an' we ain't here to mo-lest no women, neither. After what we just shown 'em, these folks ain't gonna give us no more trouble. Once we searched the place for weapons, an' this Anderson guy, we kin head back, I reckon."

Back of him the other gunmen murmured low-voiced, resentment in their hard-bitten faces. Not a man of them questioned the order, though. Fletch, the grey, moustached Wade, and the rest ducked their heads in grudging assent. Watching, Anderson sensed their wary respect for the slim, dark-featured man in the buckskin coat, and felt a little of that respect rub off on him. This Sharrock *hombre* wasn't one to be taken lightly, and that was a fact.

In front of Sharrock, Amarillo breathed out fiercely and turned away, settling the shotgun into the crook of his arm as he used both hands to roll himself a cigarette. Behind him the white-garbed figures of the angels lowered their weapons, starting to grin and shrug as the tension passed. By now Turk and Jimmy and the gunhawks they headed were into the huts upslope, crash of overturning benches and the shattering of clay utensils carrying to those below as the homes were ransacked and their meagre belongings hurled out into the mud. Under threat of the remaining guns the villagers stayed quiet, the handful of white-garbed men and the women in their flowered skirts huddling together in silence as the sack went on. Unarmed and helpless against the killers of their loved ones, only their dark eyes and sullen faces showed the hatred they felt. Drawing on his cigarette, Amarillo scanned those faces, and began to smile once again.

"Hey, Lee!" The shout came from the tall, greying *hombre* in the double-breasted shirt, the man Sharrock had named as Wade. "You figure they're gonna find anythin' up yonder, maybe?"

"Not a chance, feller." The black gunhawk shook his head, impatience creeping into his voice. Sharrock looked on disgustedly as threadbare clothes and paltry sticks of furniture were flung out of the ransacked huts, the gunmen kicking and trampling their way round the interiors as they searched for guns, or for hidden fugitives. "Way I hear it, this Anderson ain't dumb. He'd know better'n to hide out in a place like this, I reckon."

He stayed watching as the bunch headed by Turk and Jimmy came back down the slope towards them, pistols dangling low and careless in their hands. That, and the bored, angry expressions on the faces of the men, told Sharrock — and Amarillo — all they needed to know.

"Ain't a goddamn thing back there, Lee," Turk Laban said. The stocky man puckered, spitting for the ground by his feet, his broad features taut with frustrated anger. "Not a gun nor a bullet hid, an' what knives they got ain't worth a light. Sure as hell seen better places in my time . . . "

"No sign of Anderson?" It was Amarillo who asked, his smile gone thin and merciless as the yellow eyes questioned. Meeting them, Laban chuckled dryly, shaking his blond head.

"Neither hide nor hair." The gunman

sleeved sweat from his brow, the brief flicker of humour passing as a frown came back to replace it. "Ain't no Anderson in them huts, nor nothin' else neither. Gonna be wastin' your time should you take a look, better believe it."

"We've seen enough," Sharrock cut in on them, his own voice tight with impatience. The gunhawk eyed the sprawled bodies in the mud, shrugged thin shoulders as if to unload the thought of them from his mind. "Took down ten or eleven here by my count, an' the rest ain't got a weapon between 'em. No way they're gonna give us trouble from now on." He turned, gesturing angrily to the men around him. "Let's go, you *hombres*! Reckon there ain't nothin' more to find!"

He had started forward, sidestepping the nearest of the bodies as he made for the far side of the clearing, when Amarillo spoke.

"We also will search their huts," the gaunt man told him. He let his cold gaze rest on Sharrock, the smile grown narrow and mean on his thin-lipped mouth. "*Quien sabe?* Perhaps we shall find tracks that your own *pistoleros* did not see."

Sharrock held that bleak amber stare for a while. Shrugged at last, turning away.

"Be my guest." The black gunman didn't sound like he meant it. Sharrock moved to sheathe the .44 Remington, others behind him gradually following suit as they realized they had nothing left to fight. Beyond them, Amarillo smiled tightly around his cigarette, and nodded to the white-clad bunch at his back.

"*Adelante, hombres!* We search the *jacals*!" He turned, starting upslope at a stalking, long-legged stride as the angels hurried to follow him. Halfway to the huts he paused, that cold look coming back to where Sharrock waited. "Afterwards, we shall burn their homes," Amarillo said. He pitched the cigarette butt away from him, the smile fading to leave his face hard and stony as before. "Let them sleep in the open, when we are gone. It will help them to remember us, I think."

He turned abruptly with the words, striking on for the sprawl of buildings with the other Mexicans close behind him. Sharrock watched them go, his thin features puckered in a scowl of disgust.

"Sure one hell of a feller to know, ain't you?" the black man murmured.

He stood, sourfaced still as he waited with one hand rested on the Remington's butt. He couldn't wait to get away from this place, with its scared *peons* and wrecked huts, and the bodies with their stink of death. Well as Gill paid, there were things that a gunman didn't do, things that came too low to be expected of him. Sharrock figured this had to be one of them.

Pity they hadn't found Anderson. That way they might have had themselves a fight, at least.

"Time to go, feller," Anderson murmured.

He edged warily back around the thick bole of the tree that shielded him from the men in the clearing, moving slowly deeper into the foliage beyond the trail. Down by the creek Sharrock and his bunch still waited, watching the angels climb upslope after Amarillo as he led them towards the huts. The dark man breathed out carefully, his lean face hard and bitter as he studied that gaunt, distant shape. He lowered his arm, sliding the Colt to leather as he went. Not a thing he could do to help them right now, he told himself. Folks in the village had suffered enough already, and it looked like they had more of it coming. No sense in sticking around to get himself caught, and making things worse for them and him.

To say nothing of Juana.

He looked to where she crouched in the shelter of the trees, and beckoned her to him. Anderson went low as the sign was given, inching his way back through the leaves and the low-hung boughs. He'd gone maybe thirty yards when he sensed the suggestion of movement close in to his left. The dark man had the knife clear of its rawhide sheath as a big, blunt-fingered hand closed over his wrist, and a familiar figure broke through the last of the ferns to join him. Anderson met the dark eyes of the *peon* woman and grinned ruefully, his grip on the knife relaxing.

"Used to think I was quiet, Juana," Anderson said. He glanced down to the strong, brown hand whose fingers still circled his wrist. "Reckon you kin let go of me now. I ain't about to hurt you."

Juana nodded, forced an unsure, shaky smile in answer. She didn't speak. Meeting her eyes again, he saw the tears that welled there. Anderson sighed, his own grin fading. For a moment, he'd forgotten that it was her people they'd watched Amarillo and Sharrock gun down. The dark man reached over, and laid a steadying hand on her shoulder.

"Take it easy, Juana. Okay?" Anderson told her.

"*Si*, Andres." Juana formed the words as a hoarse, choking sound. The woman shook herself free of his hold, brushed her wet eyes defiantly with the back of her hand. "I am ready now."

She moved ahead of him, leading the way deeper into the dense growth of lianas and fleshy-leafed boughs that shut them off from sight of the watchers in the clearing. Back of her Anderson sighed again, his dark face grown sombre as he recalled the bodies of the villagers sprawled in the mud, the dying yells of the *federales* mown down in their makeshift pirogues. Amarillo and his bunch had one hell of a payment coming to them, and that went for Sharrock too.

He only hoped he'd be around to collect.

He plunged forward, following her lithe shadow-shape into the green mass of foliage beyond. Anderson ducked his way under creepers and whipping branches, careful to keep his footing on the unsure bed of moulds and leaves. About him raucous cries of birds and other slithering movements told of the non-human life that filled the trees around him. Down by his feet he sensed a shivering of undergrowth, and some unseen thing flowed over his moccasin toes like a swiftly uncoiling whip, flicking away into the bushes on the far side. Anderson grimaced, breaking stride for an instant. Just as well he couldn't see everything, he thought.

Behind them, from the clearing, fresh cries and wailings sounded, and with them a lower, rumbling noise. Crash of collapsing buildings, and fire taking hold. Halting to look back, the dark man saw a rolling mass of smoke shot through with brighter spouts of flame, that now lifted above the open ground, bathing leaves and tree-boles with a tawny, fitful glare.

That bastard Amarillo had fired the village!

Far ahead of him, into the thickets, he caught the tremor of foliage as Juana came to a halt, looking backward to the clearing. From here he couldn't see her face too well, but he figured he could guess the expression it was wearing. Reek of burning carried to him on the heavy, listless air, stink of straw and bedding, of nets charring in flames, and the sickening stench of roasting fish. Anderson shook his head against it, leaned to spit into the bushes. He turned from the rolling pall of smoke, moving quickly to where Juana stood half-hidden in the ocean of green, waiting for him to catch up with her. By now he figured they were out of immediate danger. Amarillo was a desert man, no more used to jungles than Anderson himself. The way the dark man saw it, neither he nor Sharrock would be likely to follow

138

tracks this far into the undergrowth, when there was a chance of their getting picked off by folk who knew the territory.

He was almost within hand's reach of Juana when he saw how she stood quiet, an upheld finger to her lips, and halted, reading the warning. Anderson kept a hold on the knife, not troubling to unship his unfired pistol. In this kind of situation, maybe the silent weapon was the better of the two. Now he looked toward the peon woman, his eyes questioning. For answer she gestured with a jerk of the head, indicating a cluster of bushes away to the right. Meeting her gaze, the dark man nodded. Ducking low beneath the leaves and ferns, he started in towards it.

A low murmur of voices reached him before he parted the nearest of the brush, as yet too indistinct for him to hear what was said. Anderson's keen ears registered them as the voices of men, separated them into three distinct fragments of sound. So he had three *hombres* to deal with, at least! He went forward cautiously, reaching to hook the last fronds aside as the sound of those voices grew clearer.

"*Andale, amigos!*" the one nearest to him called to the others. There was no mistaking the urgency behind his words. "Quickly, my friends! There is not much time . . . "

Peering through the last of the shielding brush, he made out the three crouched figures in the narrow space between the walls of jungle foliage. They were all digging frantically to unearth something from a fresh-turned pit in the ground, their backs toward him as they worked. One, he noticed, used only his right hand to claw at the earth, his left dangling awkwardly with a blood-splotch staining the white cotton sleeve. Eyeing the *peon* clothes, the rope sandals and straw *sombreros*, Anderson nodded. These were the three he'd seen make a break from the clearing a short time before.

Even as he watched, the bunch of them drew out a heavy, bulky bundle that was swathed in what looked to be an old tarp. It rattled faintly as they set it down, the objects it held rolling to spread across its weathered surface. Before he looked, Anderson reckoned he knew what it contained.

He eased his way through the clinging leaves, and stepped into the open. "Easy, fellers," the dark man murmured. Then, recalling his Spanish, "*Amigo, hombres. Soy amigo.*"

The short, thickset Mexican nearest to him was the first to turn, his burly frame tensing as he darted a hand down for the half-seen objects in the tarp. The other two were ready to follow suit when the stocky *hombre* froze halfway through the move, his broad, moustached face breaking into a grin as he caught sight of the man in front of him.

"*No tiran*, Ernesto!" this one ordered. He laid a hand over the wrist of the big, grizzle-headed Mexican alongside

141

as the *hombre* made to lift a pistol from the sheet on the ground. "This one is a friend."

Up above them Anderson stood stooping beneath the overhang of brush. He, too, had begun to smile. "Damn if it ain't Tortuga!" The dark man shook his head, unable for the moment to believe it. "What in the hell are you doin' here?"

"It is my home, *señor*." Catching sight of the reflected glow of flames on the trees behind him, Tortuga let his smile grow fainter for an instant. "At least, it was before these *ladrones* put it to the torch." Recovering himself, the short man shrugged, looking to Anderson and back to the men beside him. "*Amigos*, meet the Señor Anderson, the one I have spoken of many times. Señor Anderson, these are my good friends Ernesto and Ramon."

"*Buenos dias*." Anderson ducked his head, still smiling at the unexpected pleasure. "Good to see you fellers, an' no mistake."

"Señor Anderson," Ernesto bowed in answer, sweeping off his huge *sombrero*. Beneath it his round skull showed bare and tanned through a grizzled tonsure of hair. "It is our pleasure."

Thin, pock-marked *peon* they called Ramon didn't speak, nodding in silence. He flexed the bloodstained arm, grimacing to the pain as he met the tall man's gaze. Anderson acknowledged the look, his own pale-eyed stare raking over the litter of weapons on the tarp. Looked like they had four Mauser rifles in there, with an equal number of pistols, plus boxes of shells. Scanning the hoard, the dark man smiled wider, reached to heft one of the short guns from the ground. Just as he'd figured — .45 Colt Army, same as the one he carried.

"Good weapons you got here, fellers," Anderson said. His smile grew sly and knowing. "You have any gun oil with 'em you kin spare?"

"*Naturalmente*," Tortuga nodded

eagerly, leaning back to seize on another of the objects inside the tarp. "It is yours, Señor Anderson, if you will take it."

"Best news I've had today," Anderson said. He held to the grin as Juana emerged from the brush on the far side, moving in to join them. "Come on over, Juana. Seems like we struck lucky here, after all."

He moved aside, making room for the woman as she hunkered down to join the group, and laid the unearthed .45 back on the surface of the tarp.

★ ★ ★

He checked the action of the freshly oiled Colt, found that it answered sweetly. Anderson nodded, weighed the pistol for balance before setting it down. The .45 Army had come through its sousing better than he'd dared to hope, and now he knew for sure it could be trusted. Pretty soon he'd be back in business.

He turned back to the squatting bunch around the open tarp, leaving the pistol bedded on his bandana alongside. By now darkness had begun to sweep over the jungle, the trees drowning in widening pools of shadow as the first stars showed through gaps in the leaves overhead. From the distance a faint crackling sound and wafting smudges of smoke told of the charred village smouldering in its ashes. Anderson listened to that sound for a moment. Frowned, shutting it from his mind. Wasn't a thing he could do about what had already happened, he told himself. Maybe, in time, the sons of bitches could be made to pay.

"How come you're here in this place?" he asked Tortuga, and the stocky man shrugged, his white smile rueful beneath the thick moustaches.

"I have lived here from a child, Señor Anderson," the Mexican told him. "I was in this place for *muchos años* before I worked for the Capitan Salazar, in Tamaulipas and elsewhere.

Maybe you are thinking of the last time we worked for him, at Laguna Roja?"

"Ain't likely to forget it," Anderson nodded, grinning wryly at the memory. "We were all of us lucky to come through that one, I reckon." He paused, looking again to the litter of weapons on the sheet. "You tellin' me these guns were stowed ready for when the *federales* landed here?"

"As you say, *señor*." This time it was Ernesto who cut in on them both. The big Mexican, though, did not smile, his leathern face sombre as he balanced one of the Mausers across his knees. "Ramon and I have also worked for the *capitan* in the past. The weapons we stored many months ago in readiness, but when the landing failed we knew we could be of no help, and left them buried — until now. *No es verdad*, Ramon?"

Ramon ducked his dark head in answer, not troubling to speak. Juana and Anderson had cleaned out his wound, and padded it with a strip of his torn shirt, and though still pale, he looked in better shape than he had a while back. Now he toted one of the Colt pistols in his right hand, and from the expression on his lean face Anderson guessed he was ready to use it on the *hombres* who had burned his village.

"So where is Salazar?" Anderson asked. It was a question that had been haunting him from the time he'd got ashore, and now the anxiety showed plain in his voice. Meeting the dark man's eyes, Tortuga frowned and spread his hands, glancing sidelong to the men about him.

"*Quien sabe?* Maybe he is already dead, Señor Anderson." The thickset *hombre* shrugged, sadness shadowing his broad, moustached features. "We watched from a distance, but the rainstorm was heavy, it was not easy to see." He looked again to Ernesto and Ramon, who shook their heads. "None of us saw him there, *señor*."

"I have seen him, Andres," Juana said.

She leaned towards him with the words, reaching to shove back the black wing of hair from her eyes. Meeting the tall man's questioning gaze, Juana nodded, a faint smile forming at her lips.

"*Verdad*, Andres. It is the truth."

"How come you didn't tell me before?" Anderson demanded.

"You did not tell me you wished to know, Andres," Juana answered him reasonably, as if speaking to an awkward child. The Mexican woman sat straight-backed, both large hands braced on her thighs. As yet, she made no move to touch the guns on the tarp before her. "I saw him living, before I found you. They took him alive, the *pistolero negro* and the one you call Amarillo."

"How'd you know it was him?"

"Amarillo, the tall one with the eyes of a cat, called him by his name. I was hiding close to them, and heard him

148

speak." Juana held the look he gave her, the threat of a smile vanishing as her face regained its former impassive calm. "The Capitan Salazar, your friend. He is a tall man, a rurale, with the unshaven face of a *bandido*?"

"Yeah, you could say that." Anderson managed the most rueful of smiles. "That's Salazar, all right. So they took him alive, an' that's the last you saw, huh?"

"As you say, Andres," the *peon* woman nodded. "Afterwards, I went further into the forest, and found you there. There is nothing more to be told."

"So he's alive, anyhow." The relief in the dark man's voice lasted only for a moment. Anderson remembered Amarillo, and the kind of treatment Salazar was likely to get as a prisoner in his hands. "Or he could be, unless the bastards have tortured him so bad he's died of that, maybe." He scowled, shaking off the thought as he looked again to the woman beside him. "Juana, you know where this settlement is, that the *pistoleros* built. Reckon you're gonna have to take me there, honey. Ain't no way I aim to let Salazar die there like a butchered hog!"

Juana didn't answer him, her smooth features betraying their unease. Instead it was Tortuga who spoke, his voice carrying to them from the far side. "That would be unwise, Andres," the stocky man warned. Tortuga spoke warily, eyeing the other's hard, determined face in the dying light. "Amarillo and the leader of the *Americanos* have many guns to call on. You will be one man against fifty or more, you will have no chance."

"Got eight guns here, ain't we?" voice of the dark man struck harshly in answer. Anderson gestured to the weapons in front of them, to his own oiled Colt on its bandana bed. "Nine of 'em if you count mine too. Oughta give some of us a chance, at least."

"Four of us, perhaps." Ernesto didn't sound too convinced. The big man glanced up to Anderson and shook his grizzled head, his face already wearing a look of resignation. "*Señor*, if you are thinking of the peons in the village, do not raise your hopes. They are fishermen and farmers, and work for Capitan Salazar as we have done. They will not know how to handle guns."

"Worse than that, *amigo*." Tortuga frowned, recollections of the burned village in his mind. "They saw how Amarillo and his friends surrounded us and gunned us down like sheep. Now, when we ask them to fight with us, they will remember."

"*Verdad*." Ramon spoke for the first time. His sullen face matched the defeat in his voice. "Four against fifty is no better than one man alone."

"So why'd you come out here an' dig up the guns?" Anderson asked.

"*Quien sabe?*" Tortuga sighed, hefting the rifle like a useless weight in his hands. "We had seen them kill our friends, and ran to stay alive. Maybe when we got here we were *un poco*

151

loco — a little crazy . . . "

"And maybe I also am crazy," Juana broke in on them abruptly, her voice hard and impatient. "I will take one of these *pistolas*. Give it to me, Andres."

At the sound of her voice beside him Anderson turned, startled for a moment out of his anger. Meeting the fierce gaze of those dark eyes he smiled, and reached for the nearest of the guns.

"Sure thing, Juana." The dark man lifted one of the Colts, broke open a box of shells to fit loads into the chambers. Anderson left an empty under the hammer, handed the weapon to her butt first. Tortuga and the others looked on in a shocked silence as she took it from him.

"I am one of the *peons* you spoke of," the woman told the watching men. She held the heavy pistol awkwardly in both her hands, its barrel pointing to the ground as she answered. "I have never fired a gun, or spilled another's blood, but the killers of our people give us no other choice. We must learn to use the guns, and fight. If we do not, the *malo hombres* will stay here and kill more of us, and we shall know no peace."

"They will kill us if we fight them, Juana," Ernesto offered.

"Not if we shoot them first," the woman told him. She gripped the .45 pistol, her look coming back to rest on the dark man nearest her. "Is it not so, Andres?"

"You said it, Juana." Anderson's grin cut fiercely into the darkness of his face. He reached out with the words, laying his hand on the bare arm that held the gun. "Reckon you said it all, lady. We got no other choice."

She didn't answer, smiling openly as her dark gaze shifted to the hand on her arm, and back again into his face. For a while they stayed that way, his eyes and hers meeting together as the silence grew harder to bear. It was the voice of Tortuga that broke it at last.

"This is foolishness, Andres," the

stocky man sighed, keeping his grasp on the rifle as he struggled to his feet. "One man, or five persons, it is the same — we have no chance. But we are *loco hombres*, we will come with you. *No es verdad*, Ernesto?"

"*Si*, Tortuga. We are with you." The balding Mexican ducked his head, his heavy features sombre in reflection. Beside him the taciturn Ramon nodded agreement, shoving the pistol into his belt.

"Best we should go back to the village," Tortuga decided. He started ahead for the screen of jungle brush, rifle held across his body as the others moved to follow. "Those who have stayed will need to be warned, if we are to find more to fight with us."

"I will speak with them!" Juana had regained her feet, a tall, commanding figure in the gathering dark. "I am not hired by the *rurales*, or the state governor. The people know that I am a *peon*, as they are . . . they will listen to me, and know I speak the truth!"

Tortuga met the determined stare of those eyes. He shrugged again, looking to Anderson questioningly.

"Best do like she says, feller." The tall man was still smiling as he bent to pick up his bandanna and the pistol inside it, and slid the weapon to the leather holster at his hip. "Reckon she knows how to handle this better'n you or me."

He grinned, tying the bandanna at his neck as the others moved to gather up the guns from the ground. Anderson was close behind Juana as she followed the three men through the foliage, heading for the sheltered track beyond. Tortuga, leading the group, had gained the fringe of the thicket and was about to step into the open, when a sound from further down the trail alerted him. The stocky Mexican sprang back, his rifle and the weapons of the rest coming hurriedly to bear as the bushes shook violently and the first of the uncertain figures stumbled into the open ground.

"*Alto, hombres!*" Tortuga shouted. "*Arriba con sus manos!*"

A short distance behind him, Anderson had his own gun levelled as the foremost of the newcomers burst into view down the trail. One look at the uniformed, dishevelled figure was enough. The dark man breathed out slowly, his gun-arm lowering to bring the weapon down. Beside him, Juana caught the move, and did the same.

"Damn if it ain't Lieutenant Ibanez." Anderson still sounded like he didn't believe what he was saying. Scanning the trail, he watched as other figures reeled out of the brush behind the leader, the whole bunch coming on unsteadily towards them with their hands raised.

"*Soy amigo! No tiran!*" the officer called out to them as he staggered forward. Now Tortuga and the others saw plainly the mud-spattered uniforms of the men who followed, and hurried to lower their rifles. Ibanez came to a halt in front of them, his boyish

156

features pale and hollow-eyed from weariness as he swayed and fought to stay upright.

"Do not shoot us! We are your friends!" Catching sight of the tall, dark-featured man who stood with the *peons*, the young officer stared, taken aback for a moment. "Señor Anderson? I did not expect to find you here . . . "

"It's me all right, Ibanez." Anderson's glance had shifted beyond the lieutenant to the troopers who followed. Seven of them in all, and the whole bunch looked to be out on its feet, far gone with fear and exhaustion, their uniforms torn and splashed with mud. Not so soaked, however, that they'd had to swim ashore, and they still held on to their rifles. From the look of it, they could still fight if they had to. The dark man signed to them to lower their hands. Turned back to Tortuga and the rest, his thin smile glinting.

"Now maybe we do have a chance," Anderson said.

5

"WE were more fortunate than the rest," Ibanez said. He picked his way along the track that lay half-hidden by the dense brush, using his drawn revolver to thrust the heaviest branches aside. "We reached the shore before our pirogue foundered, and in the storm they did not find us. Others that we saw were not so lucky, Señor Anderson." He paused for a moment, glancing back to the tall man who followed him. "You saw Captain Aguirre, before you escaped?"

"Aguirre's dead. I saw them kill him in the marshes." Anderson's stony face betrayed nothing of what he thought. He stayed close behind the young officer, Juana with him and the seven *federales* bringing up the rear, as Tortuga and his friends led the column

158

back towards the village. About them dusk deepened through the trees in rich hues of purple and gold, the jungle filling with the restive movements of night creatures and the cries of roosting birds. Last of the fading light picked out the spirals of smoke that still rose from the smouldering village ahead. The way that they were going.

"Only other *hombre* still alive is Salazar, an' word is he's a prisoner in their camp, far side the island. I aim to get him out from there, Ibanez."

He caught the look of startled surprise on the lieutenant's smooth features, and nodded.

"That's right, *teniente*." The dark man's face was a shade harder than before, the pale eyes holding a grim, determined light. "We're gonna break out Salazar, an' settle with Amarillo an' the whole bunch. This time, though, we're gonna do it right. *Entiende?*"

"Señor Anderson?" Ibanez's voice tried to sound both puzzled and offended, and didn't quite make either one. "I am not certain that I understand you?"

"You know what I'm talkin' about, right enough," Anderson told him. His bleak gaze touched on the officer as he spoke. "This time it's gonna be my way, Ibanez, the way it should have been at the start of this mission. You ain't in command here, any more'n Aguirre was, you hear? We already seen what come about when he tried runnin' the show, an' now we're pickin' up the mess he left us. It ain't gonna happen again, okay?"

"If you say so, Señor Anderson," the youngster answered stiffly, resentment plain in the sound of his voice. Anderson ignored it, ploughing brutally on.

"Damn right I say so, an' you better believe it!" The outburst seemed to rid him of the last of his anger, and the dark man sighed, his tone gentling. "Okay, Ibanez. So none of this is your fault, I know that. Fact is, Juana here an' those *hombres* up ahead are callin' the shots right now. They know the country, they know where Amarillo an' his pals have their camp, they have weapons for eight takers, an' Tortuga there claims he knows where the villagers have pirogues hidden, should we need 'em." He broke off, eyes still on the man in front as he paused for breath. "We're gonna need their help, Ibanez. Seems to me we best be ready to take their advice too, don't you reckon?"

For a while the young officer made no answer, his smooth features set hard as he moved unsteadily forward through the brush. Then the thin shoulders relaxed, the stiffness going out of him, and he ducked his head in agreement.

"You are right, Señor Anderson." For the first time Ibanez's voice betrayed the utter weariness he felt. "It would appear that we have no other choice."

"That's all I wanted to hear, feller," the dark man told him.

His glance left the youngster, cutting back behind himself and Juana to the men who followed. The seven troopers moved forward in silence, their broad *Indio* faces heavy with weariness, their bowed shoulders sagging. Bone-tired and sullen from what they had been through in the past couple of days, they stumbled awkwardly along the narrow trail, clutching their rifles as though the weight of the weapons held them upright. Scanning those blank, hollow-eyed faces, Anderson frowned. Ibanez had brought along eight more guns, but the unit was in a poor state right now. What was coming was likely to take most of them beyond the limit of their endurance, and could prove too much for them in the end. The dark man breathed out slowly, turning from them. Like Ibanez had just said, they had no choice. No way they could leave the island in safety until they'd settled with Amarillo. It would be Anderson's job to make sure this bunch were tough enough to see it through.

From close beside him, Juana caught his eye, and smiled. "We go to my people now, Andres," the woman said.

She reached over and gripped his left hand, squeezing it reassuringly. "After what has been, it will be better. *Verdad?*"

He met the dark, level stare of those eyes, heard the determination in her voice, and figured that Juana was the strongest of them all.

"*Gracias*, Juana," Anderson said. He returned the pressure of her hand, forced an answering smile he didn't altogether feel. "Could be you're right."

She loosed hold on him, shifting both hands to grip the heavy pistol, and the two of them went ahead in silence as the last fringe of thickets gave way to the village.

The clearing no longer showed its sprawl of makeshift dwellings. Anderson breathed in the burning stink of wood and fish, eyeing the wreckage of what hours before had been a village with a life of its own. Charred ruins of log cabins met the look, smoke wafting from inside the gutted shells, their leaf and sod roofs fallen in and flared away to ash; collapsed skeletal ramada frames, remnants of smouldering nets, the scattered bodies of pigs and dogs in beds of smoking ashes where *jacals* had stood. Anderson felt his mouth dry out like a year-old hide, a taste like a brass cartridge case lying heavy on his tongue. The dark man turned his head and spat away to the ground, but the sour, metallic taste stayed with him.

The surviving villagers had returned some time before. Now they stood in a dejected crowd by the crest of the slope, with shoulders hunched and heads bowed. The men had removed their straw *sombreros*, and one — the *viejo* that Amarillo had seized, when the gunmen had surrounded the place — seemed to be speaking to the rest in a low, subdued tone. Drawing closer, Anderson saw that some of the *peons* held wooden shovels, and that the crowd was grouped around a series of freshly-dug graves. Tortuga and his friends were already climbing the slope as the oldster finished his prayer and the villagers crossed themselves. They had almost reached the makeshift cemetery when a young child saw them coming and tugged at its mother's skirt, calling out.

"We have come back, Porfirio," Tortuga said.

He came to a halt a few yards from the burial-place, setting his rifle butt to earth as the startled bunch of villagers turned to face him. Anderson saw smiles touch the faces of some as they recognized Juana and the other three, but they lasted only a moment. Most of the *peons* were already looking to the tall, dark man in the hunting-shirt and denims, and the travel-stained unit of *federales* with the young officer at their head. Meeting those wary, suspicious glances, Anderson sensed that this wasn't going to be easy.

The old man had left the side of the newly-made graves. Now he came forward to where Tortuga waited, his withered features clenched tight in sudden anger. "You come back here with guns?" Rage shook his voice, threatened for an instant to prevent him from speaking. Porfirio glared at the thickset man, pointed with a trembling hand to the wrecked village, the fresh grave mounds behind him. "Do you not see what they have done to us already? You have lost your mind, Tortuga! If they come back here and find you with guns in your hands, they will kill us all!"

"Not if we kill them first, *viejo*," Anderson said.

Sound of his voice cut through the sobbing of the women, the suspicious mutterings of the men. Hearing, Porfirio frowned, his glance shifting from Tortuga to this stranger who stood beside a smiling Juana, the .45 Army filling his hand.

"Who are these *extranjeros* who come with you, Tortuga?" the oldster asked.

"I am Anderson. The one they look for," the dark man told him.

He saw the stunned expressions on the faces of the villagers as the words were spoken, the shock that turned rapidly to outraged anger. Anderson didn't wait for them, aware all eyes were on him as he spoke again.

"Juana would have brought me here, to hide from the *pistoleros*," Anderson said. He met the fierce gaze of old Porfirio, his own features stony hard. "We were close to the village when they came, we saw what was done here. At that time we could not help, but now we have guns, and are ready to fight." He paused, glancing back to the group of armed figures around him. "There are thirteen of us, and we have weapons for three others. If you help us now, we can win."

"When all the *federales* came, you could not win." Porfirio's voice had lost its anger, his wrinkled face taking on a look of weary resignation. "Señor, we have eleven graves behind us. We were helpless when there were more of us than there are now. If we dare to

167

fight so many, they will leave none of us alive."

"And if we do not fight, they will leave none of us alive!" Juana thrust forward from the group, her voice angry and impatient. Her outburst cut through the last of Porfirio's words, the muttering peons struck to silence as the tall woman dared them with dark, blazing eyes. "I also saw the killing, and the tall hombre with the escopeta, the one called Amarillo. He would have butchered all of us, if the negro had not prevented him. In time, he will think again, and come back. What will you do then, Porfirio? Do we fight, or wait for them to cut us down like the sheep we are?"

She broke off, her broad bosom heaving as she fought to get back her breath. In front of her Porfirio stared uncomprehendingly, shocked out of speech by what he had heard. Behind him the crowd murmured among themselves, glancing uncertainly one to another. Juana seemed not to notice them, ignored them together with Anderson and a startled Ibanez as she launched herself into a second fierce tirade.

"There will be more killing here, before this is over!" Juana shouted. The sound of her voice rang through the open space, echoed back from the surrounding trees. "If we help Andres and these others, we may live afterwards to look each other in the face without shame. I have never used this pistola on another, but if I must, I will do it. If there must be death, let us be sure that we do the killing, and are not the ones who die!"

In the momentary silence that followed she breathed heavily, her anger spent, and turned to the dark man beside her. At the admiring look on his face, Juana smiled again.

"Attagirl, Juana," Anderson murmured.

He glanced back to the restless group of villagers, who had now begun to argue loudly among themselves, one or two voices carrying above the rest.

169

From what Anderson could make out, it wasn't Juana who was the target of their anger, but Porfirio.

"She is right, old man!" A hard-favoured, haggard-looking woman shouted from the head of the bunch, thrusting out her hand towards Tortuga, who held one of the spare pistols. "Give me a gun, I will fight! They killed Honorio, who was my only brother. If there are no men among us, we will avenge our dead!"

She left the group in a fierce, darting lunge, snatching the pistol from Tortuga's hand. Behind her others came hurriedly forward, their hands stretching for the guns that remained, as the noise of the crowd grew louder.

"Do not fear, Epifania!" one of the men called out to her. "Some of us are not ready to be sheep for these butchers! We will fight also!"

Most of the clamouring bunch rushed forward, grabbing for the guns. In a matter of seconds the remaining weapons had new owners, who moved to join the dishevelled group around Juana and Anderson. A few, more uncertain than the rest, stayed back, looking questioningly to Porfirio, who shook his head sadly in defeat.

"And what are the rest of us to do, without guns?" the oldster asked.

"We will take more of them from the ladrones!" It was the hard-faced woman, Epifania, who called out again in answer, her black eyes harsh with anger as she brandished her newly-acquired pistol. "They will not expect us, after what has happened, and we shall find weapons for those who are left. Is that not so, Señor Anderson?"

"That's right, lady," Anderson grinned tightly, his look still with the old peon in front. "Stick with us, Porfirio, an' we're gonna come out on top, I reckon. What do you say?"

For a moment the viejo held his gaze, not answering. Then Porfirio sighed, shrugging his shoulders in acceptance.

"You give me no choice, Señor

Anderson. I must take your side." The watery eyes of the Mexican appraised the dark man thoughtfully as he spoke. "It will be for you, though, to answer for those who die."

"I know it, Porfirio," Anderson nodded, his harsh features sobering. His glance left the old man, raking over the other waiting figures about him. "Okay, folks. Best we move out at first light, if we aim to take these hombres by surprise."

"*Un momento*, Anderson!" Tortuga's shout broke in on him suddenly, turning his head around. The stocky Mexican frowned, glancing to Ernesto and Ramon as the dark man's look came to rest on him. "We have eyes and ears downriver, *amigo*, from the time Salazar sent us to work. The latest word is that a shipment of guns and supplies comes to the island in two days, from a landing-stage nearer the coast."

"You don't say?" All at once the tall man's eyes were alight, keen and wolfish in the dark Indian face. "Guns, Tortuga? Did I hear you right?"

"As you say, *amigo*, guns and supplies." Tortuga nodded eagerly, his own broad features betraying their excitement. "What they tell us also is that within the month, more men will come *Quien sabe*? Maybe more guns with them."

"How many with the shipment?" Anderson wanted to know.

"A small escort. No more than eight men."

"And how far off is this landin'-stage you're talkin' about?"

"A half-day's journey, amigo. That is all."

"*Esta muy bien*, Tortuga," Anderson said. He called out to the waiting *peons*, his voice cutting sharply across the clearing. "Okay, you *hombres*. You heard what he just said, more guns downriver in two days' time. Come the night, most of us will be out of here to pay 'em a visit. Once we have more guns, we'll be back, an' that's when we smoke out this hornet's nest far side the island. You folks gonna give us a hand, or not?"

Shouts of agreement rose from the huddled crowd, and Anderson found his smile. He was still grinning as the officer of *federales* plucked at his sleeve, concern in his boyish face.

"Señor Anderson, is this wise?" The youngster sounded troubled. Ibanez stole an uneasy glance at Juana, at the hard-featured Epifania, both toting their guns. "To give arms to women, in such a place . . . are these people to be relied upon, do you think?"

He saw the bleak, cold stare in the tall man's eyes, and fell silent.

"Told you before, they're the one chance we got." Anderson spoke curtly, impatience in his voice. "Gonna have to trust 'em, Ibanez, an' that's all there is to it." He paused then, beckoning the stocky Tortuga over towards them. "Let's go find these pirogues you got hid, feller. Looks like we might be able to use 'em real soon."

"*Seguro*, Anderson. *Con mucho gusto*," Tortuga grinned, hurrying over. The thickset Mexican pointed to the thickets beyond the clearing, eagerness in his voice. "If you will follow me, *amigo*."

He, Ernesto and Ramon set off for the edge of the clearing, one or two of the *peons* following. Anderson was set to go after them when he sensed movement beside him, and turned to find Juana looking his way.

"It has gone well, Andres," the woman said.

"Sure has," Anderson told her. His glance went over her with the words, taking in the tall, firmly sculpted shape of her, wide-hipped and full-bosomed in the blouse and patterned skirt. Anderson studied the strong, calloused hands that gripped the gun, shifted his gaze upward to the broad Indian face with its dark-eyed stare and the black, gleaming mane of hair that overhung her brow. He nodded at last, still impressed. "Seems to me like you're

175

one hell of a woman, Juana."

"If you say so, Andres." Her smile grew warmer, the dark eyes probing him more closely than before. "I said only what I believed to be the truth."

"So you're comin' with us, huh?" He reckoned he knew the answer.

"How can I stay behind?" The dark gaze held his, the warmth of the smile grown slyer by a shade. "I am with you in this thing, Andres. I shall not leave you until it is over. Now go with Tortuga, he is waiting."

Her smile stayed with the dark man as he turned from her, following Tortuga and the others to the far side of the clearing.

★ ★ ★

"Straight flush wins!" Jimmy Wagoner laid his cards face up on the dirt floor one by one. The thin-faced gunsel raked in the pot, his crooked grin widening as he studied the disgusted expressions of the players around him.

"Thanks a lot, boys. Sure is a pleasure to take your money!"

"Lucky sonofabitch, ain't you?" Turk Laban scowled resentfully, eyeing the worthless hand he'd just scattered in the dirt. "Ain't had me a halfway decent hand all night."

Squatted alongside him by the corner wall of the bunkhouse, Christie and Goddard said nothing, their sullen faces testimony enough of what they thought. Wagoner seemed not to notice them, the lopsided grin still splitting his thin, unshaven face as he sat back and scooped the winnings into the derby hat he held in his lap.

"It's called talent, is all," the gunman told them. Wagoner eyed the mound of coins and dollar bills inside the hat, nodded appreciatively. Gill paid good money, and they'd been playing for a while. Must be close on five hundred in there, he figured. "Talent is what I got, fellers, an' there ain't no answer to it, you hear?"

"Talent for fixin' a deck, maybe."

177

Goddard spoke for the first time, his deep voice rumbling to echo off the walls. The huge, bearded man looked to Wagoner, accusation in his dark, piercing eyes. "Helps a man win a hand, from what I heard."

The heavy silence that came after hit the place like a drench of icy water, the group of players freezing motionless. Beyond them, the dozen or so other men sharing the log-walled bunkhouse halted what they were doing, glancing warily towards the bunch by the corner wall. For a while, it was kind of hard for a man to breathe.

"You callin' me a cardsharp, Fletch?" Jimmy Wagoner's voice was down to a hoarse, choking whisper. The thin, leather-faced *hombre* set down the derby hat and the money it contained, his blanched features taut on their bones as he wiped sweating palms on his thighs. "By God, you better take that back, an' be mighty quick about it."

"An' if I don't?" The bearded giant

178

lifted himself to a poised crouch that took him halfway to his feet, his massive right hand hovering low by the butt of the holstered .44 Dragoon. "What in hell you gonna do about it, Jimmy?"

He was set to move backward and make his play when another hand seized on his gun-arm with a grip that bit tightly into the bunched muscle of the biceps. Goddard grimaced, turning his head, and met the cold stare of Wade Christie. The grey-haired gunhawk shook his head slowly, and Fletch Goddard let out a harsh breath, unclenching his hand. Far side of them both, the barrel-chested Laban called out to Wagoner as the thin man reached for the gun at his hip.

"Leave it be, God damn it!" the blond gunman shouted. Laban struck the other's hand from the gun-butt, his broad features harsh with anger. "It's but a card game, ain't it? You fellers gone *loco*, or what?"

"He didn't mean nothin' by it." Christie's voice struck as chill as the look in his eyes. The tall *hombre* released his hold on Goddard's arm carefully, still holding the bearded man with his pale, steely gaze. "That's what he was just gonna tell you. Ain't that so, Fletch?"

"Yeah." Goddard spoke the word as if red-hot pincers had torn it from him. Meeting Wagoner's white, convulsed face, he shrugged awkwardly. "Didn't mean nothin' by it, Jimmy. No offence, feller. Okay?"

"Could be I'll overlook it the once." The thin-featured man's voice was still bitter and unforgiving. Wagoner sank back on his haunches, clutching the derby as his look raked over the huge man who faced him. "It better not happen again, though. You hear me?"

Goddard didn't answer, sullen-faced as he nodded.

They didn't hear the bunkhouse door come open behind them as the other two hombres ducked their way inside. First warning they had was the thudding sound as it hit back against the wall, and the hard, steely voice that called out to them.

"Evenin', fellers." Lee Sharrock stepped forward with the words, stalking his way down the bunkhouse to the group at the corner wall. Behind him the short, thickset figure of Bradley Gill quickened his pace in a vain attempt to catch up alongside. Though the black gunman smiled, his eyes scoured the other men with their dark, probing stare. "You boys got somethin' to tell me, maybe?"

"Wasn't nothin', Lee," Wade Christie said.

He stayed where he was, standing beside the glowering figure of Fletch Goddard as they both turned to face the newcomers. On the far side of them, Laban and Wagoner scrambled hurriedly to their feet, the thin *hombre* still clasping his overloaded hat.

"Just havin' us a hand of stud," Wagoner glanced cautiously towards the black gunhawk, his voice apologetic for once. "No harm in that, I reckon."

"Is that right?" Sharrock's smile grew tighter by a notch. The small, buckskin-jacketed figure let his own gaze shift from Wagoner, and back again to the tall, grey-haired Christie. "Seems to me you boys been havin' some kind of a dis-agreement over these here cards, an' that ain't what I call healthy. You take my meanin'?"

Christie met the hard, jetstone stare of those eyes, and bit down on the instinctive flare of anger. He was the fastest gun in the bunch, adept with either of the twin, short-barrelled Smith and Wesson .44s he carried in the *buscadero* gunbelt around his hips, but against somebody like Sharrock he hadn't a prayer and he knew it.

"Whatever you say, Lee," the tall man murmured.

"Glad you see it that way." Sharrock kept to the last of his smile, his gaze touching on the other three men in the group. "As it happens, we got just the thing to keep you *hombres* out of mischief. Ain't that right, Mister Gill?"

"That's right, Lee." Bradley Gill sounded impatient. The thickset, undersized man stuck his thumbs into the armholes of his vest, drawing himself up as tall as he could. Even so, he didn't quite reach the ear of Sharrock, who next to himself was the smallest man in the room. "We have a job for you men, and it won't wait. The shipment we've been expecting from the coast is due in the next couple of days, and we can't afford any mistakes. The weapons and supplies it carries could be the difference between us living like kings out here, or the whole business turning sour." He halted, scanning the hard, untrusting faces that surrounded him from above. "I need to make sure that they arrive here safely, and you boys are going to help me. I'm detailing Lee here to take a picked squad downriver at first light, and rendezvous with the shipment."

"Fifteen men, an' you four hombres are first on my list," Sharrock cut in sharply, almost interrupting the stocky man beside him. The black gunhawk had regained his vicious smile, not bothering to turn his head as he called to the other watching men behind him. "Stover! Heenan! You an' the rest git your gunbelts on an' be ready to move out. What's in this place oughta be enough for the job."

"Sure thing, Lee!" The answer came back hurriedly from the group further back, men hustling out of their bunks to strap on their weapons. Over by the corner wall, meeting that dark, mean stare, Wade Christie nodded in agreement.

"Guess we're ready too, Lee," the grey man said. Catching the angry pebbled gaze of the stockier figure on him, he touched the brim of his hat respectfully. "Same goes for you, Mister Gill."

Gill didn't answer, his prim mouth pursed tightly in annoyance. He had begun to take exception to the way Christie and the others ignored him, seeming to listen only to what Sharrock had to say. Thinking it over, it seemed to Gill that the black man had come in a little too soon a moment ago, when he'd barely finished speaking. Maybe he'd have a word with Sharrock later. After all, the sonofabitch was only a couple of inches taller, and black into the bargain. If Napoleon had been in charge around here, he sure wouldn't have let it pass.

"Sure you gonna be safe while we're gone, Mister Gill?" Big Fletch Goddard asked. The bearded man eyed his paymaster coldly, the sneer plain in his voice. "How 'bout that greaser feller, Salazar? He got loose one time already, ain't that right?"

He saw Sharrock look briefly in his direction, and scowled, falling quiet. Goddard turned away for his bunk, gathering up his belongings as Laban followed and Wagoner hurried to transfer his winnings to the money belt at his waist.

"Amarillo has him under guard, and is taking personal responsibility!"

Bradley Gill clenched his grip on the armholes of his vest, his jowled face a deeper shade of red as his voice grew shrill and tight. "Salazar will not escape again, and his security is none of your business! What I want from you — all of you — is a good job done, and no mistakes. Is that understood?"

Grudging murmurs of agreement answered him, and the stocky businessman nodded, halfway satisfied by the response.

"That's better," Bradley Gill breathed out, his stubby hands unclenching. He turned from them, heading for the door. "Just be sure you remember, that's all."

He made it to the open doorway, went through at a short-legged strut to vanish from sight. Grins came briefly to a few weatherbeaten faces, disappeared rapidly as Lee Sharrock looked them over.

"You heard him," the black gunhawk told them. "This shipment don't git here, we could find ourselves without shells, an' with nothin' to eat neither. That gits to happen, I git mad, an' you *hombres* are gonna be sorry. You savvy?" Scanning the silent, chastened faces that met him, the slender killer nodded. "Okay, boys. Out from here inside the hour, an' git ready for some hard rowin'. We're headed downriver!"

He turned away with the words, the others watching as he moved for the door beyond.

6

HE dug with the paddle into water that was black and thick as molasses, felt the weedy growths slither off the blade as it struck and came free. Anderson grunted with effort, sweating hard as he dug for the water again. This near to the coast, the river shrank to a brackish, salty channel overgrown with mangrove thickets, whose tall stems arched above them to shadow the water. Pale flowers showed against the fading darkness, white blotches on the black tangle of roots and stalks that hemmed them in from either side. Oppressive heat pressed down on them in spite of the dark, bodies streaming wet as they fought to drive the pirogues forward. Sweat showed as a black, spreading stain across the broad plough-horse shoulders of Tortuga, who crouched on the thwart in front of him, the soaked shirt clinging to his back as his powerful muscles stretched and heaved. Behind him came Juana's gasp of effort as she struck with the rest, the narrow pirogue sliding through weed-choked shallows for the channel's mouth that now showed a paler light through its black arch of mangrove stems.

There were five pirogues in the water, each holding five men or women in its narrow length. Besides himself, Juana and Tortuga, Anderson's boat had a couple of *federales* aboard, who answered to the names of Oomez and Padilla. The second held Lieutenant Ibanez and three more troopers, with the burly, grizzled Ernesto at the prow, while Ramon headed the third with a crew of the veteran Sergeant Pena, trooper Musquiz, and two *peons* from the village. The last two boats were crewed entirely by the villagers, a youngster called Mario leading the fourth, and a withered-looking oldster by the name of Jorge bringing up the rear. Each of them held two *peons* armed with pistols from the cache, one of them the hard-faced Epifania, who rode in Mario's craft. That way, no single pirogue was manned by an unarmed crew, and each one had a leader who knew the river and its dangers. It was Tortuga who deserved the credit for it. He'd planned the whole expedition from beginning to end, and Anderson figured he couldn't have picked a better man for the job.

They'd left the village that night, not troubling to wait for the passing of darkness. Way Tortuga saw it, first light would be too late, bringing them to the place when the sun was high and the escort awake and ready for a fight. By leaving that night, a good time should get them to the landing-stage before dawn, hopefully with most of the gunhands in their bunks. Thinking it over, Anderson had seen no other way to play it. He'd left Tortuga to pick enough crews for the five pirogues, and ensured that the remaining weapons were passed around. Porfirio and the rest of the villagers they'd left behind, in the ruins of their homes. The oldster had told him they aimed to lie low in the thickets while the daylight lasted, and by the time dark came again the five boats should have returned with more guns. Either that, or Anderson and the others would all be dead, and it wouldn't matter anyhow.

They'd struck out around the far side of the island, avoiding the camp of the Anglo gunmen and Amarillo's angels, and skirted the fringe of the swamp, making downriver for the coast. Now, with the darkness slowly fading, he knew they must be getting close.

Sweat slithered down his forehead, stung into his eyes. Anderson sleeved the moisture from his face, blinded for an instant as he struck for the water. Recalling the *peons* left behind, the dark man frowned. That had been the toughest part of it, leaving those people unprotected, if only for a few hours. Thought of old folks, and women and children, fending for themselves in that jungle, with Amarillo and his friends still running loose, bothered him even now. He sighed, pushing the unwelcome thought to the back of his mind as he brought the paddle clear. Right now, there was no better way of helping the *peons* than what they were doing. Fixing the shipment, and laying their hands on more weapons, was the only chance they had.

Sure, it was a risk. Sure, if things went wrong they could lose all their guns and their toughest fighters in a single shoot-out. But the way things stood, they didn't have much of a choice.

In front of him Tortuga turned his head, glancing swiftly over his shoulder to the rowers at his back.

"Not far now, Anderson," the Mexican told him. Tortuga grinned fiercely, his black hair and moustache glistening with sweat. "Just beyond the channel's mouth. Tell them to be ready."

He turned away before the taller man

could answer, digging his paddle hard for the black water. Anderson was still passing the word along to the others when a sudden shout sounded from one of the pirogues further back, and the whole flotilla halted, the crews glancing behind them as they shipped their oars.

"More pirogues, *amigos*!" It was the old man, Jorge, who called, from his place at the rear of the column. The Mexican pointed back upriver to where darkness and overarching mangrove stems all but hid the water from sight. "We are being followed."

A low murmur threatened from the other *peons* in the rearmost boats, that stilled as Tortuga lifted his hand for quiet.

"How far, Jorge?" the squat man asked, and Jorge shrugged, uncertain.

"I do not see them, Tortuga. I hear their paddles at a distance." The oldster frowned in thought. "*Quien sabe?* Maybe two hours, maybe more."

"How many of them?" Anderson

wanted to know. This time Jorge shook his head.

"They are too far, *señor*. I cannot tell their numbers."

"*Gracias*, Jorge," Anderson said. His glance moved to Tortuga, who had again turned to look backward. "Seems we have to move faster than we thought, *amigo*. What is your word?"

"As before. We follow the river on its near side, and strike from the shadow." The Mexican no longer smiled, his broad features grim beneath their coating of sweat and mud. "There is an inlet close to the landing-stage, with mangroves that should give some cover, at least." He paused, glancing to the pirogues that waited behind them. "Have them follow closely, and stay quiet."

From the seat at his back, Juana looked towards him. Anderson met that questioning stare, his lean face hard and determined.

"This is it, girl," the dark man told her. He called out to the others, cupping his mouth with his hands. "Okay, *amigos*! Stay close, an' have your weapons handy! We're goin' in!"

He hoisted the paddle, the five of them striking together to send the slim craft forward, the sound of other dipping oars coming after as the crews of the remaining boats hurried to follow.

They'd been rowing for maybe another hour, and darkness was paling away in greyish streaks above the water, when Tortuga slid his paddle clear and the pirogue glided out from the last of the mangrove arches. Ahead of them the river broadened to a huge open span, the shoreline curving outward as the tangled thickets gave back. Bend of the river formed a smooth, stagnant pond at the near bank, with small inlets that probed into the mangrove fringe. Far side of the pool, a wooden landing-stage ran up to the shore, and a couple of heavy, flat-bottomed barges were moored to posts set into the mud. Beyond the makeshift jetty two log-walled buildings stood silhouetted against the trees, one of them with a loading bay leading down to the water. Bunkhouse and storehouse, Anderson figured. More mangrove thickets followed the river in its winding curve, pressing closer along the banks as it went on to merge with the Laguna Madre, and the coastal marsh of Tamaulipas.

Tortuga gave the sign to start rowing, and he dug with the rest, their paddles slicing smoothly into the water. The stocky Mexican led the pirogues into the open, hugging the mangroves on the near shoreline as he made for the cluster of buildings and the landing-stage ahead. The towering wall of the planted roots loomed above them, its shadowing darkness covering the boats as they edged forward in line astern. When they gained the inlet closest to the landing-stage, Tortuga turned in among the mangroves, ducking his head to the trailing boughs and their pale yellow flowers. Deep into the sheltering thicket, he roped the pirogue's prow to the nearest of the rough-barked trunks, and laid his paddle in the bed of the boat, picking up his rifle. The thickset man eased himself over the side and into the water, standing waist-deep with the rifle above his head. Signing for the others to follow, he started back for the mouth of the inlet as the four pirogues and their crews slid cautiously into cover behind.

Anderson hoisted the unbuckled gunbelt from down by his feet, clasped it left-handed as he unsheathed the .45 Army with his right. He followed Tortuga over the side of the boat and into the murky water of the inlet. Black, slimy tide lapped him to the waist, and the dark man grimaced, holding the pistol clear of the mangrove shoots on either side. The gunbelt he slung at his left shoulder, holding out his freed left hand to Juana as she clambered after him out of the pirogue. The Mexican woman leapt from the boat, her wide skirts billowing as she hit the water. He caught her against him in the moment she landed, and for a while she stayed close, pressing her body to him as her bare brown arm circled his neck.

"Later, Andres," Juana said. Her eyes looked levelly into his as she spoke.

He didn't answer, his throat gone suddenly tight, uncomfortably aware of the warmth and closeness of her body, and his own instinctive response. Aware, too, that what he was feeling wasn't altogether uncomfortable either. Then the *peon* woman slipped her arm from his neck, and struggled back along the shallow inlet with her soaked skirts dragging heavy behind her. Anderson went after her, the *federales* following as the crews of the other pirogues made their ropes fast and stepped into the water.

Soft, clinging mud slowed their progress, the weight of the murky water pulling them back as they stumbled on half-buried mangrove roots in the bed of the inlet. By the time they emerged from its entrance they were all sweating hard, and Tortuga let them halt to regain their breath before moving on again. The squat Mexican led them single file around the curve of the shoreline, still hugging the shadow of the mangrove wall as they trod the muddy shallows. No sound of patrolling guards broke the stillness, no sudden challenge from the bank. Gripping the heavy .45, planting his moccasined feet carefully in the slippery mud, Anderson nodded grimly. Looked like they weren't expected here.

He and Juana were close behind Tortuga as they reached the moored barges, ducking swiftly to cover in water that rose to their chests. Scanning the open ground beyond the landing-stage, they saw no movement from the buildings, or into the nearby trees. Tortuga grinned, turned to beckon the others forward. He was still signalling to them as Anderson and Juana left the water and went in at a headlong run for the nearer of the two log-walled cabins, guns lifted in readiness.

Anderson gained the near wall of the building, bracing himself against the rough-hewn logs as he fought for breath. Juana reached the wall a moment after, the heavy pistol toted in both hands. She leaned there beside him, heart thudding as she recovered from the headlong dash from the water's edge. Anderson grinned as reassuringly as he could, signed for her to follow. The dark man started to inch his way along the wall, making for the corner and the door that lay beyond.

The sentry had been out behind the storehouse, taking a leak. He came in around the far corner of the wall behind them both, his rifle cradled easily across his body, smoke curling from the cigarette in the side of his mouth. Anderson didn't see him until the *hombre* had his weapon halfway lifted, and then it was Juana's sudden shocked gasp that warned him. Too late, he started turning to meet that

200

carbine's muzzle as it came level on him at the waist . . .

Low hissing sound struck from behind them, something tearing the air past Anderson's face. The long-bladed knife thumped into the sentry's chest, sank itself almost to the haft. The gunman reeled backwards into the wall, eyes staring fixedly at the handle that jutted from his bloody shirt. He fumbled at it, trying to pluck it loose as he slithered down the wall, the carbine slipping unfired from his hands.

Anderson felt the thudding vibration as the sentry hit the wall, heard the sound of voices from the cabin. He didn't stay to watch as Tortuga came up with them and hauled his bloody knife from the dead man's chest. The dark man launched himself at the door, smashing it back on its hinges to plunge inside. Shadowy gloom of the interior hit him, and the reek of sweating bodies packed close together. Anderson glimpsed the moving shapes that told of men rolling off makeshift bunks and grabbing for their guns. Called out, his voice cutting harshly in the crowded room.

"Don't try it, fellers! We got you treed!" the dark man yelled.

He saw one figure lean out from his bunk, snatching for a hanging belt, and swung to trigger a shot. The bullet ploughed into the log wall by the gunman's face, stung him with flying splinters. Noise of the shot blasted around the room, and the *hombre* dropped back howling, one hand clutched to the gashes in his cheek. Either side of him, outlines of other men froze to the sound.

"That's better," Anderson told them. He stepped aside as Juana slid in at the open doorway, Padilla and Gomez close behind with their rifles levelled on the men in the room. "Now you boys stay nice an' quiet, an' don't nobody make a move for his gun. Next time I don't aim to miss."

His eyes growing more accustomed to the darkness of the room, he ran his gaze over the bunch in front of him. Anderson counted seven men and nodded, satisfied for the moment. Eight with the sentry. That meant they had all the shipment's escort right here in the bunkhouse.

"Hey, mister!" one of them called out to him, sounding aggrieved. "What in hell you doin', givin' a gun to that woman yonder? She's like to kill us all, holdin' it that way."

Anderson said nothing, hiding his grin with the back of his hand. Beside him Juana drew herself to her full height, her face stern behind the heavy gun. "Then you had better not offend me, *hombre*," Juana said. "Otherwise you may die by the hand of a woman, and that is not a good thing to write on your grave."

Behind her more *peons* filled the doorway, shoving their way inside. The dark man started back towards the door, his gun still levelled as he drew Juana after him.

"Padilla! Gomez! Keep 'em covered!"

203

Anderson told the federales in the room. He beckoned the waiting *peons* forward. "You fellers tie these men — use belts, bandanas, whatever rope you kin find. Make sure you rope 'em good, an' bring their guns out with you. We're goin' to the storehouse."

He backed out through the door and into the paling half-light, Juana close by him. Tortuga was outside, pushing the wiped knife into his belt. Seeing the dark man he grinned fiercely, brushing the sweat from his eyes.

"So far it goes well," Tortuga said. He eyed the taller man carefully.

"You are not hurt, my friend?"

"Not a scratch." Recalling the sentry, and the carbine muzzle, Anderson grinned ruefully. "*Gracias, amigo*. He almost had me there."

"*Por nada*." Tortuga glanced to the water's edge, where Jorge and a group of *peons* were busily staving in the barges with heavy rocks. Behind him, young Mario toted the sentry's carbine as two other men dragged the body

204

away into the trees. "Now there is only the shipment. *Verdad?*"

"Yeah." Anderson peered anxiously into the far reaches of the mangrove-walled channel, knowing he wasn't going to see much in that tangle of boughs. "That, an' the fellers behind us, whoever they are."

He saw the look the stocky Mexican gave him, and nodded slowly. "Guess you're right, Tortuga," Anderson said. "Reckon we know who they are, all right." He turned, heading away from the cabin and towards the larger building with its loading bay. "Let's go see what they brought up from the coast."

He reached the storehouse as a charging rush of *peons* and *federales* smashed the door off its hinges and hurled it down with a booming crash inside the building. Following them into the gloom, Anderson saw that the walls were lined with stacked crates and boxes, some of them covered over with burlap sacks. Ibanez and his men were first to them, the young lieutenant shouting directions as Musquiz splintered the lid of a crate with his rifle butt, and Sergeant Pena broke a second open with his booted foot. Watching, Anderson saw the veteran rip back the oilskin covering to reveal a case of gleaming, polished rifles. Pena glanced up to his commander, and smiled.

"Find the shells, *andale*!" Ibanez told him. He whirled on the remaining troopers, pointing to the other boxes. "Seguin! Benitez! Open the others, quickly. We do not have much time!"

"There are supplies too, *teniente*!" Musquiz called out from where he bent above his opened crate. "This holds no guns, only coffee and beans."

Standing on the flattened door in the open space it left behind, Anderson looked on as Ramon and Epifania led a mob of *peons* in a rush for the remaining crates. Presently the air resounded to the crunch of splintering wood, and the harsh screech of nails ripping loose from the planks. Soldiers and villagers grabbed at the weapons and goods inside, sometimes struggling among themselves as they pulled them free.

"Take what you kin carry, folks!" Anderson shouted. He glanced back uneasily behind him, at any moment expecting those other pirogues to appear in sight. "What we can't take with us, haul outside an' dump it in the swamp! We don't want it gettin' into the wrong hands. *Entiende?*"

Catching his eye, the grizzled Ernesto nodded. He and a handful of *peons* seized on a couple of the untouched crates, lugging them towards the door.

"Señor Anderson!" Ibanez sounded shocked. The officer looked towards him, reproach and anger in his tone. "What you are doing is the wanton destruction of property, maybe the property of this government. *Señor*, I must protest . . . "

"I call the shots here, remember?" the voice of the dark man hit back at

207

him, tight and hard in the confines of the room. Anderson raked the officer with his bleak, wolfish stare, his Indian features harder than stone. "That's the way your government wanted it, an' that's how it's gonna be. *Sabe Usted?*" He nodded to the oncoming *peons*, moving aside to let them pass. "Okay, fellers. Just do like I say."

He watched them out through the doorway, heard the heavy splash as the first of the crates hit the water. Back inside the storehouse, they had finished ransacking the supplies they needed, villagers and federales all toting extra guns and boxes of shells, and more than a few carrying coffee and sugar inside their shirts.

"Good work, amigos," Anderson told them. He grinned as Ernesto and the others came back, gasping from their recent exertions. "Just a couple more to go, I reckon."

Tortuga came in through the gap as Ernesto and his bunch dragged out the last of the crates. The stocky man held his rifle by its sling, and his broad moustached face still held its savage grin.

"What are your orders now, Señor Anderson?" the Mexican asked.

He glanced towards Ibanez as the words were spoken, and for a moment the face of the dark man thawed, hint of a smile quirking the lips. Then it was gone, and the sombre expression returned.

"Got somethin' in mind for those *hombres* that are followin' us," Anderson said. "If it works, it oughta take care of 'em, but we'll need to move fast." He paused, glancing again to the group of *federales*, and their scowling officer. "*Teniente* Ibanez! Take your men, and come with me! We have work to do!"

He turned on his heel and went out through the door, not looking behind as the troopers hurried to follow. Outside by the water's edge another echoing splash told of the last crate being hurled into the swamp. Ducking through the doorway, he caught the questioning gaze of Juana beside him. Anderson met that look, sober-faced.

"Now we will have real fighting, Juana," the dark man said.

★ ★ ★

Sunlight hit the flat span of open water ahead of him, struck the surface to a tawny gold. Sharrock leaned back, easing his stroke as the rest of the crew slowed with him. Heavy, moist heat pressed down on the men in the three pirogues, sent the trickles of perspiration coursing over faces and bodies. Sharrock brushed at his dripping brow, sank his paddle again as the boat glided across the pool for the landing-stage. He'd been right to pull out before first light, the black gunhawk told himself. Sun was already fierce enough, with the day hardly begun. A couple of hours later, and they'd have suffered a whole lot more.

His glance cut back to the men who rowed behind him, their sweating faces clenched and intent as they leaned and struck for the water. Wagoner was with him in the first pirogue, with Turk Laban in the second. Goddard he'd put into the last, with the grey-haired Christie to watch him. After what had happened in camp, he figured it made sense to keep Goddard and Wagoner apart. Sharrock let his look touch on them, and turned back to the oncoming shore. Seemed kind of quiet out here, he thought. No sign of any guard, and he could almost feel the weight of the silence on his shoulders. A way quieter than it ought to be.

"Hey, Sharrock!" Jimmy Wagoner's voice broke the stillness, carrying plain over the flat stretch of water. The scrawny gunman in the derby pointed shoreward, a startled expression on his gaunt, unshaven face. "Sharrock, somebody sunk the goddamn barges! Looks like they been stove in!"

The black gunhawk heard that voice, heard the sudden fear that shook behind the words. Sharrock followed the pointing finger, saw the hulks of the moored barges close to shore. They were still roped to their posts, but now both of them foundered low in the water, their splintered planks letting in fresh surges as they sank gradually beneath the surface of the pool.

He'd guessed right the first time. It *was* a way too quiet, after all. "Head for the bank!" Sharrock yelled to the other men in the pirogues. He flung down his paddle as his own craft neared the land, clawing the .44 Remington from the holster at his hip. "Some bastards got here before us, men! Let's go smoke 'em out!"

He lunged from the boat, landing knee-deep in the muddy, shallow water. Lee Sharrock fought his way to the bank, hearing the floundering splashes as others leapt overboard behind him. The small man led the rush up the narrow beach, the bunch close after as they ran for the shelter of the bunkhouse. Plunging awkwardly through the soft, clinging mud, Sharrock found time to wonder why no shots had come at them as they landed. Why the landing-stage and its buildings still lay silent as the gunmen came within yards of the bunkhouse door.

Lashing sound of bullets cutting air, and the cries of stricken men around him warned him of a trap that had been sprung. Sharrock flung up an arm to shield his face as the ground seemed to erupt into gouts of flame-stabbed smoke, deafened by the shattering roar of the volleys that smashed into them from behind and to the left. About him men lurched and went down, the guns spilling uselessly from their hands. To one side he caught sight of Jimmy Wagoner, his pale face savage as he lifted the old Starr Arms pistol for a shot. Second volley blasted the thin-featured gunman, catapulting him backward as though he'd been hit by a sledgehammer. Wagoner struck earth with a racking thud, his own gun exploding under him as he rolled to lie still. The derby hat flew from his head, landing upside down as if to catch the money that filled the belt around his hips.

A close-ranged slug ripped through Sharrock's buckskin jacket, tugging at his arm in passing. He swore as a second bullet grazed the side of his face, still searching for a target. Now he could see the men who reared up from the rifle-pits they'd dug in the ground some distance from the shore. The group of uniformed *federales* with their young officer, lining their weapons for another killing volley from the rear, while white-clad *peons* fired on them from the flank. Sharrock snarled, triggered into the smoke where he'd seen a gunflame a moment before. His shot kicked a uniformed trooper back against the wall of the pit, the rifle clattering from his grip as he reeled and slid down from sight. Sharrock barely had time to register the hit, a murderous volley blasting from the rifle-pits to bowl more men from their feet. Beyond him, a handful of gunmen gained the bunkhouse as fresh gunfire hammered into them from loopholes in the wall, tearing them down.

"Let's git from here, damn it!" Sharrock bellowed.

He swung away from the riflemen in the pits, darting past the two loopholed buildings for the cover of the trees. Shots kicked dirt behind him, and the fierce hornet-whine of a flying bullet sang close by his head, but Sharrock kept going, legs driving hard as he covered the muddy ground. Back of him came a stricken yell, and the thump of a falling body. Sharrock ignored it, stumbling and almost going down in his haste to gain the trees. He made it to cover as the last shots cracked behind him. Christie, Laban and Goddard were with him as the survivors plunged deeper into the sheltering foliage, but not so many more. Less than half of the men who had landed got clear of the beach.

Anderson saw the handful of gunmen

break past the rifle-pits and head for the trees. Crouched in the thickets that covered any approach to the left of bunkhouse and storehouse, the dark man nodded. He'd been counting on something of the kind, and that was why he'd kept the small group with him in reserve, while Pena and Ramon directed the fire from the buildings, and Tortuga and Ibanez led the riflemen in the pits. Juana was in cover beside him, and further back the bushes gave shelter to the grizzled Ernesto and Epifania, with Mario, Jorge and a couple more. Now they looked to him as the gunmen struck for the jungle ahead, eager for the word.

"Let's go!" Anderson shouted.

He broke cover, leading them forward at a run. The dark man didn't head after the fleeing gunmen, turning to strike left on a parallel course through the thickets. Anderson ploughed his way through the ferns and the boughs with their glossy leaves, struggling to clear a path for the rest. If he had it right, Sharrock and the others would be turning to come in on their flank pretty soon, and that meant that his bunch ought to meet them halfway.

He fought his way out from the nearest thicket that brought him nearside of a clearing, Juana and the *peons* hurrying to follow him. Anderson signed for them to take cover on either side, lapping the rim of the clearing in an outflung line.

The dark man dropped to one knee behind the nearest trunk, using his left arm to steady the Colt as he brought the weapon level on the open ground.

Sharrock and the others came into sight almost as he made the move, outlines of their bodies etched plain in his vision as they crossed the spaces between the trees. Anderson watched the lithe, buckskin-clad figure edge gradually closer, scanning the dark boles warily as he led the other gunmen in towards the clearing. Anderson counted six men behind the black *pistolero*, waited until the whole group were inside the open stretch before calling out to them.

"Throw down the gun, Sharrock!" Anderson yelled. "We got you cold!"

He'd already known that the little *hombre* was fast, but the speed of Sharrock's reaction took him by surprise. The black gunhawk lined and triggered the .44 Remington in one rapid move almost as Anderson began to speak, the bullet ripping bark from the tree-bole above the lawman's head. Anderson ducked from instinct as sap and bark-shards rained on the back of his neck, shooting blind. His slug, too, went high, plugging the wide-brimmed hat from Sharrock's close-cropped hair. The small man dived across the clearing, already running as the other guns cut loose, the ragged volley blasting back from the surrounding trees.

After Sharrock, Christie was the quickest to his guns. The grey-haired man had both Smith and Wesson pistols cleared and stabbing flame as the shooting started, and the hail of slugs mowed down a *peon* rifleman to Anderson's right. Ernesto led a volley that raked the clearing, his own shot smashing into Christie's chest and spinning him halfway round to hit the tree behind him. The grey-haired killer staggered, tottered forward, still trying to lift his guns. Roar of the volley took him down, plunging headlong to earth. Behind him, Mario's shot slammed a second man over backwards, his arms flinging wide to the impact.

Boom of a heavy pistol racketed across the clearing, the slug whipping close by Anderson's shoulder. He was lining to shoot when Juana fired, wincing as she braced herself against the kick of the heavy .45 she gripped in both hands. Fletch Goddard had Anderson in his sights when Juana's slug struck him, and dashed the smoking Walker Colt from his hand. Numbing force of the bullet shocked him, froze him for an instant against the pain as it hammered him off his feet. The huge, bearded gunman hit the ground hard, struggled briefly to rise. He fell back, groaning, clutching a bloody shoulder that felt like it was busted.

"I got enough, goddamn it!" Turk Laban shouted. The blond, barrel-chested man threw the gun away from him, hurrying to raise his hands. Around him, those who still lived were doing the same. "Don't shoot, you *hombres*! We just quit!" He stood, his broken face sullen in defeat, hands still lifted as the last echoes of the shooting died away, and Anderson and the rest broke cover with their guns levelled on the men in front. Ernesto spared a glance for the crumpled figure of the *peon* in the bushes. He looked to Anderson, shaking his head.

"Pepe is dead, *amigo*," the grizzled man told him.

"Pity, Ernesto. He was one too many to lose." Anderson studied the bunch of prisoners facing the guns, the two who sprawled silent in the grassy clearing. "Two dead, one wounded, an' more who look like they've taken enough. You done a good job, fellers." He turned from the heavy-set Mexican, sheathing the Colt as he started at a loping run for the far side of the clearing. "Make sure they stay put, Ernesto. I'm goin' after Sharrock!"

He moved away, ducking low against the tree-boles as he rounded the edge of the clearing, heading for the thickets beyond.

"Andres!" Juana's voice came from further back, a sudden unease in the sound. "Andres, wait! He will kill you!"

He didn't answer. Didn't even look around. Wall of jungle met him, and he dived into it, hauling the first of the heavy-leafed branches aside.

Once inside the dense mass of foliage, he went ahead as swiftly and quietly as he dared, burrowing low through the creepers and fronds with his ears straining to catch the slightest sound. The gun he kept holstered, knowing he would need both hands to get far in this overgrown stretch of jungle. The dark man set his feet down lightly, thankful for the moccasins that deadened the noise of his footsteps over the jungle floor. Again he didn't follow the gunman's trail directly, striking parallel to come in on him from the side. Sharrock didn't know this country any better than Anderson did. Way the lawman saw it, he'd likely take the first cover that offered, and wait for them to come to him.

He clawed through the next couple of thickets, staying low and ducking his head to the lashing boughs. One branch more tensile than the rest whipped on the back of his hand to leave red welts behind, and Anderson bit on his lip to stifle the cry of pain. He went ahead, coming out from the thicket on his belly, watching for any movement to the right. First sight that met him was a massive deadfall, hanging halfway to the ground in a smothering mass of creepers. Beyond it, another fallen tree made a gap in the foliage, thickets fringing the tree-boles on either side.

This is where he'll be, all right, the dark man thought.

Anderson edged from the thicket on hands and knees, went out around the first deadfall and into the bushes, working his way to the right.

Sharrock lay flat behind the ragged tree-stump, levelled his pistol on the open space beyond. From here he figured he had a clear sight of whatever was coming after him, and chances were they'd have to cross the open stretch by the deadfall to get at him. He doubted there was a man in that bunch capable of sneaking through the thickets without him hearing something. The black gunman scanned the jungle ahead of him, eyes hard as jetstone in the narrow ebony face. That must have been Anderson who called out to him back in the clearing, the gunman thought. Looked like the sonofabitch was tricky enough, with the rifle-pits and all. Tricky enough to take the shipment escort, and fifteen picked gunmen into the bargain. But he didn't have Lee Sharrock's skill with a handgun, no sir. And if he came ahead now, Mister Anderson was due to find out just how big a mistake he had made.

Sudden dart of movement in the thickets warned him, brought him swiftly alert, his dark eyes intent on the jungle ahead. Sharrock smiled coldly, steadying the .44 Remington so that its muzzle covered the fringe of the thicket that lay to the right of the deadfall, the place from which the first tell-tale movement had come. He was still watching as the nearest of the bushes shivered and burst open, and the Mexican woman plunged into view, looking desperately about her as she steadied the pistol in both hands.

Back of the stump, Sharrock's cold smile faded, the black gunman frowning uncertainly as he studied the figure over the Remington's sights. Sharrock was not a woman-killer, and didn't mean to be if he had the choice. But when a woman came hunting him through the thickets, with a gun in her hand . . .

Sharrock swore softly under his breath. He started to his feet, lining his pistol on the woman's waist as she stumbled into the open ground.

"*Hola, mujer!*" the gunhawk called. "*Abajo con la pistola!*"

From the corner of his eye he glimpsed another sudden move, and saw the unsure outline of a figure breaking from the thicket on his right, covering the ground between them in a rapid, diving lunge. Sharrock swore again, whirled swiftly to meet it with the gun lifting in his hand. This time he was way too late. Anderson ploughed into him like a maddened buffalo, his shoulder slamming the gunman's belly as he grabbed and flung him over to the ground. The force of the dark man's rush threw both men down, thudding against the bunched grass. Anderson caught the descending wrist as the gunbarrel hacked for his head, wrenched the arm sideways and down.

Sharrock yelled in pain, his fingers opening, and Anderson beat his hand in the dirt until the gun slid clear. He kept his hold on the gunhawk's arm, rolling aside to twist the limb up Sharrock's back as his free hand sought for a grip on the other man's neck. Sharrock tore free, aiming a head-butt backward at the dark man's face. Anderson grunted as the hard skull slammed his cheek, grabbed Sharrock's leg as the smaller man fought to scramble after the gun. He dragged the gunman back along the ground, grabbed his shirt to pull him upright. Anderson sidestepped a kick aimed at his kneecap, slammed a heel into the back of Sharrock's leg, sledging him off his feet. The black gunhawk got in one vicious punch in falling, and Anderson gasped as the blow numbed the bicep of his left arm. He dragged Sharrock's head down, ripped his right fist in an uppercut to the face. Sharrock grunted to the power of the blow, already going slack. Anderson fell on top of him as he hit the floor, smashed a second right against the gunman's chin. Sharrock gasped and sprawled out to the impact, wheezing for breath as he lay helpless, fighting to recover his senses. Above him, Anderson got up slowly, collecting the fallen gun.

"You're sure as hell a hard man to track down, Sharrock," Anderson said. He grimaced at the return of pain to his punished arm. Side of his face, too, felt like it was growing the mother and father of a bruise. He pushed the Remington into his belt, drew the sheathed Colt to cover the man on the ground. "Looks like it's over now, though, don't it?"

"You'll be Anderson, right?" The black man spoke thickly through bruised, swollen lips. Meeting his eye, the lawman nodded.

"That's right. I'm Anderson." He sensed the oncoming figure of the woman to his right. Smiling in reassurance, he beckoned her to him. "It's okay, Juana. Got him between us, I reckon."

"I followed . . . I was afraid that

he would kill you . . . " Juana's voice trembled, the pistol shaking a little in her grasp. Meeting the dark man's gaze, she too smiled, in relief it seemed. "You saved my life, Andres. I will not forget."

"No more'n you did for me, back in that clearing," Anderson reminded her. He signed with the gunbarrel to the man on the ground. "All right, Sharrock. Let's be goin'."

"Just what you aimin' to do with me, feller?" the black gunman wanted to know.

"You'll find out soon enough," Anderson told him.

Tortuga and Ibanez were waiting for them when they returned to the beach. By now *peons* and *federales* had finished stripping the dead men of their guns, and stood grinning and jubilant as Anderson and his group came out from the thickets, prodding their five sullen prisoners in front of them. For a time the dark man didn't smile in answer, scanning the sprawled, bloodstained bodies in the stretch between the rifle-pits. Nine of Sharrock's gunhands had died in the murderous volleys at the water's edge. With the other two in the clearing, that left only five from sixteen, and one of them wounded.

"Musquiz was killed," Ibanez told him. The boyish face of the officer showed a momentary regret. "There were no other losses."

"One more," Juana broke in, her voice sadder than before. "Pepe is dead."

A brief silence fell as the victors looked one to another. Some of the soldiers and *peons* had begun to eye the prisoners thoughtfully when Anderson spoke again.

"This was well done, *amigos*," the dark man told them. "The shipment is seized, and eleven of our enemies killed. We have guns and supplies for others in the village, and what we cannot carry is destroyed. Now we must go back to the island, and settle with those who are left."

"You aim to take on Bradley Gill, feller?" Sharrock chuckled disbelievingly, shaking his head. "You have to be crazy, Anderson. He must have more'n thirty guns on that there island, an' that ain't countin' Amarillo an' his bunch!"

"You had fifteen guns here, remember?" the dark man reminded him. "Seems to me they come off second best." He paused, looking over the heavily-armed group of *peons* and soldiers that waited at the water's edge. "When we hit that camp, we're gonna have more guns, Sharrock. An' I reckon friend Gill won't be expectin' us, neither. We'll finish the job, right enough."

"And what are we to do with these *cabrones*, Anderson?" Ernesto jabbed his carbine in the direction of the prisoners, his eyes murderous on the slight buckskin-clad figure at their head.

"Not a thing, Ernesto," the dark man told him.

In the shocked silence that followed,

he turned again to Sharrock. "You're a man-killer, Sharrock," Anderson said. "Could be you gunned down friends of ours these past few days, an' any other time I'd stand to see you hung. But I saw you save the old folks in that village, when Amarillo would have butchered them, an' I ain't forgotten it. That's why I ain't already shot you like a dog, better believe it."

"So what you got in mind, Anderson?" Sharrock's voice was wary, unsure for once.

"We're leavin' you here," Anderson said. Hearing the angry murmurs of those around him, he ignored them, pushing on. "Your guns are goin' with us, but we'll leave you food, an' a couple of your pirogues. You want to stick around an' wait for the *federales*, that's your business. Was I you, Sharrock, I'd head for the coast just as quick as I could make it. An' I wouldn't come back."

"What if we come after you, feller?" the gunman asked.

"Follow us, an' you're dead meat," the dark man told him. Anderson eyed the black *pistolero* sternly, impatience in his voice. "What you got here is a chance, Sharrock. You got any sense, you'll take it."

For a moment the black jetstone gaze locked with him. Then the gunman shrugged, ducking his head.

"Maybe I will, Anderson," Lee Sharrock said. He studied the other's lean, harsh face as if seeing it for the first time. "Thanks."

He and the other disarmed gunmen stayed where they were, watching as Anderson's group moved to join the men at the water's edge.

"Tortuga! You an' your men bring out the pirogues!" Anderson glanced to the three craft that rested on the beach, and nodded. "We'll take one of these, too. Should help us with the weapons an' supplies." Catching the outraged expression on the face of Lt Ibanez, the dark man shrugged. "What else you reckon I shoulda done, huh?

232

Ain't no room in the boats we got for twelve prisoners."

"Even so, Señor Anderson . . . " the officer began. The other's raised hand held him to silence.

"Just tell me 'bout it afterwards, all right," Anderson said.

"He spoke of a Bradley Gill, Andres." From closer to him, Juana's voice questioned. Turning to her, he saw the uncertainty in those big dark eyes. "You have heard of this one, perhaps?"

"I reckon." The harsh face of the lawman grew sombre as he spoke. "Ain't him I'm worried about right now, girl. It's Amarillo I got in mind, an' what he's likely to do to Salazar before we get back." Easing the .45 to leather, he signed to the waiting men in front. "Okay, you *hombres*. Let's go!"

"Andres?" This time he saw another kind of question in her eyes. Meeting it, Anderson cracked the wryest of smiles.

"Later, Juana," the dark man said.

He led the way for the shallow water, the woman following as Tortuga's men rowed the pirogues from the shelter of the mangroves, and pointed them shoreward.

7

THE sentry had no chance from the start. Ears closed to the stealthy tread of moccasins behind him, he awoke to the danger too late to make it count, his head half-turning as the gunbarrel slammed down to cave his hat over his eyes. Anderson caught him as he fell, dragged him backwards into the nearby thicket. There he used the *hombre's* belt to lash wrists and ankles together, and gagged him with his own bandana. The dark man tugged a pistol from the sentry's coat pocket, studied it a moment before tucking the weapon into his belt. Smith and Wesson 'Russian' .44. Could be worse, he figured. He burrowed back out of the thicket to pick up the guard's fallen carbine, and started in towards the camp.

Finding the place had been easy

enough. Juana and the other villagers knew it well, and had come with him most of the way. They'd returned to the island as dusk came down, working back around the mangrove swamps along the coast to meet up with Porfirio and the rest close to the village. They'd left five men with rifles to protect the old ones, the women and the children. The others had come with Anderson, crossing the island to encircle the outlaw camp in the darkness. Now, as that darkness greyed once more to early morning, Ibanez and his six surviving *federales* and more than thirty armed *peons* lay waiting behind their rifles and pistols for the order to attack. So far, it hadn't come.

That was down to Anderson. The dark man had told them to stay back, while he went in alone to find Salazar.

Around the huge compound the log buildings lay quiet, no sign of life as yet outside. Anderson took a slow, steadying breath, and stepped into the open, the carbine held across his body as he skirted the perimeter at an unhurried walk. Brush had been cut back from the outer edge of the camp for ten yards or more, and there was no cover offering itself. Best to take a chance, and get in closer. With more than thirty gunhawks in those sod-roofed shelters, Anderson was willing to bet they didn't all know each other too well. He was counting on that to get him through until he found Salazar. After that, he figured it wouldn't matter.

Across the far side of the compound a man ducked out from one of the *jacals*, a gaunt, whiskered *hombre* in a red flannel undershirt and yellow galluses that overhung his pants. He looked to Anderson as the dark man neared the buildings this side of camp, frowning uncertainly. Anderson grinned and lifted a hand in greeting, and the *hombre* turned away, bending to souse his face in a bucket of water outside. Nothing to worry him for now, but pretty soon others would be coming out. The lawman tightened his grip on the carbine, edging closer to the first of the buildings. Any way you looked at it, he didn't have too much time.

Thoughts of Bradley Gill came to mind, and his harsh face turned stony. Anderson had never met the man, but he'd sure as hell heard of him. Way he recalled it, Gill had run south when a bank collapsed, taking most of the *dinero* with him. He hadn't been heard of since, but the tale was that the money went higher than a hundred thousand dollars. Remembering the massacred *federales*, the dead villagers in the ruins of their homes, the dark man scowled. Seemed like Gill had bigger ideas than before, buying Sharrock and an army of hired guns to set himself up as some kind of warlord in Tamaulipas. The bastard had blood on his hands, all right. And if Anderson had his way, Gill would pay for it at the end of a rope.

Gill, and Amarillo.

At thought of that one his breath came

harder, rage tightening the muscles of his chest. For a moment he halted, fighting off the rush of murderous thoughts called up by that name. No way he needed telling about Amarillo. The mean-gutted, poisonous sonofabitch had been his worst enemy for as long as Anderson could remember. He'd tried to kill the lawman a dozen times and failed, but Amarillo wasn't the kind to give up easily. The half-breed stored up every last ounce of hate like snake venom, waiting for the chance to use it on the man who had so often thwarted his plans. Fact that Anderson was a half-breed himself seemed to make it more personal between them.

That was why he was holding on to Salazar, the dark man knew. Amarillo was out to make Anderson suffer before killing him, and Salazar was one of the lawman's closest friends. Hurting him would be the next best thing to hurting Anderson himself, and Amarillo wasn't likely to pass up that kind of chance.

Anderson drew a shuddering breath,

hands easing their grip on the carbine he held. Better to put that kind of thought from his mind, the dark man decided. Clear thinking was what he needed here, if he was going to be any use to Salazar. Or anyone else.

He remembered Juana, when he had told them he must go on alone. The way she had seized on his hands and held him, as if unwilling to let him free. And how she had looked at him with those dark, beautiful eyes.

"Only come back, Andres," Juana had told him. "I will be waiting."

The dark man sighed impatiently, shook himself as if coming out of water. No time for anything like that, Anderson told himself. Afterwards, maybe, it might just be different.

Always supposing he lived to see it.

He was almost to the first of the *jacals* when one of the buildings caught his eye, standing out from the rest. The shack that stood third along from him on this side had an open doorway, and a white-garbed Mexican leaned up against the log wall outside, his carbine beside him as he touched a lighted match to the corn-husk *cigarillo* in his mouth. *Hombre* was a stranger to Anderson, but the dark man figured they didn't need to be introduced. Only Mexicans in *peon* clothes inside this camp were Amarillo's angels, and this one looked like he was guarding something — or someone. Stepping forward at an easy stride, Anderson found time for the thinnest of smiles. He could stop looking now.

He had found Salazar.

Moving at the same unhurried pace, he crossed behind the first three *jacals*, and came in around the side wall of the last, holding his carbine forward. The Mexican guard turned as he rounded the corner of the building, startled by the dark man's sudden appearance. He had one hand on the grounded carbine as the black muzzle of Anderson's weapon came to rest a few inches from his belly.

"*Buenos dias*," Anderson said. He

jerked his head towards the doorway of the shack, grey eyes cold in the darkness of his face. "*Adelante, hombre.*"

He reached to grab the standing carbine, flung it out behind him. Anderson was close on the Mexican guard as the man ducked back inside the doorway, too shocked for the moment to take the cigarette from his mouth. He shoved the carbine-butt in the angel's back as they crossed the threshold, and the man staggered, tripping to fall headlong. Peering against the gloom of the enclosed space beyond, Anderson made out the two white-clad figures seated by the far wall, and the taller shape — also in white — who rolled out of his serape on the hard earth floor, one hand stretching for the grip of his sawn-down shotgun.

"Don't try it, Amarillo!" The dark man's voice cut viciously through the silence, freezing the moving hand halfway to the gun. Anderson eased the muzzle of the carbine gently sideways, covering the men by the wall. "Same goes for you *hombres*, you hear? At this range, I don't miss."

"You cannot hope to get from here alive, Anderson," Amarillo said.

He got up carefully, letting the shotgun lie as he rose to his full height, stooping a little against the low roof of the shack. Gaunt face of the half-breed showed no trace of fear, his yellow eyes challenging the man behind the carbine as his mouth twisted to an unpleasant smile.

Anderson didn't answer him. By now, he'd seen Salazar.

The captain of *rurales* sat in the middle of the floor, close to Amarillo. Until now his darker clothes had hidden him from Anderson, but as Amarillo spoke he lifted his head, meeting Anderson's gaze with a feeble, pain-racked smile. Salazar's face showed white and pasty, shining with sweat, his leather shirt and cords spattered dark with blood. Both hands had been bound in front of him, and Anderson

243

sucked in a fierce breath as he saw the bloody mess that Amarillo had made of the right hand, with each nail torn from its socket.

"He tried to escape, Anderson." The gaunt man spoke the words almost mockingly, those amber eyes daring Anderson to make a move. "It was necessary to teach him manners."

He caught the sudden killing rage that sparked in the pale eyes of the lawman, and made to dodge aside. Vicious speed of the carbine butt beat him, the blow thudding hard to the side of his head. Amarillo managed a short, wheezing grunt, then crashed like a lopped oak to hit the floor. Almost in the moment he went down, another voice sounded from outside the building.

"Amarillo?" Anderson sensed the unease behind the single word. "Amarillo, *que pasa*?"

Movement broke the darkness of the open doorway behind them, another white-garbed figure looming in through the gap. And with the flicker of white, the duller, deadlier gleam of a pistol drawn from leather. Sudden appearance of the newcomer jarred the other angels into action, both men by the wall reaching for their belt-guns as the third Mexican scrambled frantically in search of cover.

"Get down, *amigo*!" Anderson yelled. He dived backwards for the floor as the words left him, bracing the carbine against his hip to fire once before he went down. Impact of the .44-40 slug hit the nearest of the two angels with murderous force, smashing him into the wall so hard the *jacal* shuddered. The man rebounded with a choking scream, blood staining the wall as he pitched over to the ground. Anderson struck the beaten dirt of the floor, wincing as shots ripped into the earth from either side. Salazar dived to reach the fallen shotgun, pinned the butt end down painfully with his right arm to hook the trigger with the forefinger of his left hand. The weapon kicked up violently at the shot, but at this range there was no way he could miss. Blast of the shotgun shook the building to its makeshift foundations, tore the fourth angel out of the doorway as it blew him apart like a sack of bloody feathers.

Second *hombre* by the wall had time for one more shot. It cut close past Anderson's face, fanning his cheek with a warm, rapid gust of air. The dark man lay flat, felt the butt of the carbine punish his shoulder. The heavy, close-range slug ripped through the angel at the chest and sledged him off his feet, hurling him bodily into the wall. The Mexican hit without a cry, slithering slowly downward. Battering echoes of the shots went from wall to wall, growing fainter as a clamour of voices broke from the camp outside.

"*Señores!*" The unarmed guard crawled towards Anderson on his knees, hands outstretched beseechingly. "*Señores, no tiran! Por Dios, señores,* do not shoot!"

"Get a knife!" Anderson snarled at

him, his dark face savage in the killing rage. "Cut him loose! *Ahora!*"

He watched as the angel grabbed one of the knives in Amarillo's belt, hurrying to cut Salazar from his bonds. The big *rurale* gasped, grimacing at fresh pain as the ropes fell from him. Salazar eyed the terror-stricken man in front of him, swung the shotgun left-handed. Sawn barrels thudded solidly on the Mexican's skull and the man grunted, collapsing to the dirt.

"Looks like you'll get by, Mig," Anderson said. He moved for the doorway, his carbine held ready as the *rurale* captain followed, toting the shotgun in his uninjured hand. "Let's see what we got out front, okay?"

Gaining the entrance, he peered cautiously outside. He was in time to see the outlaw camp in turmoil, with gunmen tumbling hastily out of the shacks as they hurried to drag on their clothes. Most were still looking helplessly about them when a shrill whistle seared the air, and a line of travel-stained figures rose from the surrounding thickets to move in slowly, encircling the camp. Watching from inside the *jacal*, Anderson saw the trapped gunhawks stare uncomprehendingly at that tightening circle around them, the lethal ring of carbines and pistols and *escopetas* that now levelled to seek a target. Not only the guns, but those who held them. *Peon* men in their white cotton shirts and breeches, and straw sombreros. Uniformed *federales*, grim-faced behind their Mauser rifles. Most startling of all, the *peon* women in their blouses and wide, flowered skirts, fierce and terrible as they clutched looted pistols two-handed to aim at the men in the open.

"The game is over, *hombres*!" Tortuga shouted. The squat man raked a fierce glance over the encircled gunmen, his moustached features unsmiling. "Draw your guns, if you wish to die! If you have sense, you will surrender."

"You heard him!" Anderson called

out suddenly from the doorway. He stepped into the open, Salazar edging out to cover him on the right with the sawn-down shotgun. "You guys are finished, an' that's a fact. We got Amarillo back here, an Sharrock's already quit. What we didn't kill out of his bunch are headed downriver without no guns between 'em, an' the shipment's lyin' in the bed of the swamp yonder." He paused, eyeing the furious faces that looked his way, reading in them the unease that underlay their anger. "You figure I'm lyin', come right ahead. These folks can't wait to gun you down."

He waited, starting to smile coldly as the bunch of half-clothed men turned one to another, arguing and gesturing among themselves.

"Just what you aim to do with us, feller?" It was the gunman in the red undershirt, his galluses still hanging loose, who asked the question.

"Gonna have to take your chance with us, mister," Anderson told him.

"You boys let Bradley Gill talk you into this business, an' it didn't work. Could be you'll be seein' the inside of a Mexican jail for a while. Way I look at it, it has to be better'n bein' dead." Meeting the angry, thwarted face of the gunhawk, he shrugged. "Your choice, feller. Any way you tell it, it's over."

"Not quite, Anderson." The voice came coldly to him, close to his ear. The dark man turned his head to see Bradley Gill inch his way around the near corner of the *jacal*, his right arm extended before him. The short-barrelled pistol he held was an Allen and Wheelock pocket gun, .32 calibre. Right now the muzzle was lined on Anderson at a point between the eyes. "Drop the gun!"

Swearing under his breath, the dark man complied.

"You too, greaser!" Gill's voice struck at Salazar. The *rurale* captain seemed to hesitate for a moment, fury convulsing his pale, stubbled features. Then his good hand released its hold, and the shotgun fell.

"That's good," the short man told him. Gill's voice shook, the ruddy face with its walrus moustache tight and clenched. Anderson eyed the white knuckles on the hand that held the gun, met the forced, unnatural smile and the cold eyes above it, and sensed the man was close to the edge. "You destroyed my work here, Anderson. You meddled with the course of destiny. But for you I could have been an emperor, another Napoleon or Montezuma." He halted to regain his breath, that tight smile still at his lips as the pebbled eyes fixed on Anderson. "You put paid to that, Anderson. But you aren't going to survive it!"

"Andres!" Juana's voice reached for him, an anguished scream that rang out across the compound. The woman fired the heavy pistol two-handed, staggered to the recoil. The bullet crashed into the logs above Gill's head as the noise of the shot racketed in the open ground, splinters of wood spraying into the stocky man's eyes. Bradley Gill yelled, flinging up an arm to protect his face, pulling the trigger from instinct. Anderson weaved aside from the gun, closed both eyes as the weapon spat flame close to his face. He grabbed at the gun-wrist, swore as the smaller man wrenched loose from him. Gill shook his head furiously, lifting his hand for a second shot.

Roar of another, heavier gun blasted through the echoes, beat at the dark man's eardrums. Bradley Gill reeled backwards to hit the wall, losing his grip on the .32 pistol. The thickset figure doubled over, sank forward with both hands clasped to the welling hole in his side. Second shot smashed into him above the heart, froze the crazed smile on his face. Gill lurched awkwardly, plunged sideways to hit the ground. He was dead before he started falling.

Anderson stood, hearing the rasping noise of his own breathing as the sweat cooled against his skin. The dark man let his glance shift to the hard-featured

Epifania, who now came forward from the rest, the long-barrelled pistol still smoking in her hand.

"This one deserved to die!" the woman shouted. She brandished the heavy gun at the men who now stood rooted, staring at her in disbelief. "He has sent you to murder our people, and now he is finished! Do you *hombres* wish for the same?"

"Listen to her, *hombres*!" Tortuga took up the call, indicating the surrounding *peons* and soldiers and their levelled guns. "We have men and women here who are fighting for their homes, their children. They are willing to die for this, *pistoleros*! Are any of you ready to die for the dollars of a man already dead?"

His challenge cut through the shocked silence that followed Epifania's outburst, echoed around the compound. In front of Tortuga the red-shirted man scowled and looked down, unable to answer. The gunhand tugged the unfired pistol from his waistband, and threw it from him. Around and behind him, other men made haste to do the same. A cheer went up from the encircling Mexicans as the weapons clattered to the ground, and the victors moved forward, herding the gunhawks together in the centre of the compound.

"Now it is over," Salazar said.

He sagged down against the near wall of the shack, pain and exhaustion overcoming him as he nursed his crippled right hand. Anderson had moved towards him, letting the carbine lie, when a lungeing shape broke from the doorway behind him, shoving him violently to one side. Amarillo snatched up the .44-40 in the same instant, a long-bladed knife in his free hand as he dived at the nearest of the *peons* in the cordon about him. The unexpected suddenness of his emergence from the shack, and his pantherish speed, took him past the men closest to him, and he was away and running by the time the first shots tore the air behind him.

"He's headin' for the water!" Anderson

yelled. The dark man gestured to the stocky Mexican who led his rescuers. "Tortuga! Ernesto! Come with me! Stay back, Ibanez, an' look after Salazar here. We're bringin' Amarillo back!"

He pulled the Colt .45 from leather, and set off at a punishing run as the two white-garbed Mexicans hurried to follow.

The pirogues were beached on a sandy spit below the camp, that led into the thickest of the mangroves. Amarillo reached the boats as the three of them started downhill after him, paused for an instant with his knife lifted. Seeing them so close behind him, the gaunt half-breed decided against gutting the other boats and having them catch up. Instead he seized on the nearest pirogue and slung carbine and knife inside, shoving it out for the water. By the time the three men gained the beach, the craft and its one-man crew were plunging into a narrow, overgrown channel that beckoned further along the coast.

"After him, fellers!" Anderson gasped the words. He was already shoving the pirogue ahead for the shallow water by the time the others caught up with him, and was the first to climb aboard. Sheathing the Colt, and grabbing the paddle nearest him, the dark man heard the harsh bark of a 'gator from the mangroves, and shivered. He and the two Mexicans struck together for the water, the long pirogue leaping forward as they quickened speed. Ploughing along the brown water of the channel, ducking the boughs and mangrove shoots, they were soon within sight of Amarillo, and gaining. Braced in the prow of the boat, Anderson watched the pursued half-breed drive his paddle at frantic speed, his gaunt face contorted with fury. Try as he might, he could not match the pace of three men rowing together, and was able only to watch Anderson and the others draw steadily closer to him.

"Come on back, you sonofabitch!" the dark man called. "Ain't no place you kin go from here . . . "

He broke off in mid-shout as the pirogue in front of him slowed, drifting to its own momentum as Amarillo let fall his paddle. The half-breed turned, hoisting the carbine to kneel upright in the bed of the canoe. Amarillo brought the weapon to his shoulder, levelled on Anderson's chest. At this short range the muzzle seemed huge as a cannon's mouth, the gaunt face behind it showing a massive bruise on the cheek where the carbine-butt had struck him. Caught with no time to move, Anderson glared back into that gun muzzle as the yellow-eyed half-breed sighted on him and prepared to press the trigger.

Heavy, thick-leafed bough hung low above the water, stretching halfway across the narrow creek. The drifting motion of the pirogue took Amarillo to meet it in the moment he took aim. It struck across his head and back in a thudding hammer blow, hurling him out of the boat. Amarillo triggered once as he went overboard, the misaimed bullet raising a geyser of muddy water. Then the gaunt figure plunged into the murky depths of the channel, weight of the carbine pulling him down. Paddling in towards him, Anderson saw Amarillo break the stagnant surface, floundering and screaming, before he sank again from sight.

Last bubbles broke in the brown, slimy water as the pirogue halted, the three of them peering down into the creek. There was nothing to be seen, the dark water shadowing any sign of life. Only the tangled roots and archways of the mangrove jungle all around, and the gators barking from their mudslides in the thickets beyond. That, and the feeble skein of bubbles that broke and dissolved away until nothing else remained.

"It is the end for him, *amigo*," Tortuga said. The stocky Mexican watched the stolen pirogue drift helplessly away from them, deeper into the mangroves. He turned to Anderson, who still peered over the side into the water. "He is a dead man, Anderson. There is no way he could live, in such a place."

"Just wish I could believe that," Anderson said.

He stayed watching the water until the last of the bubbles were gone.

When they got back to the beach, the welcoming committee was waiting for them. Running the pirogue in through the shallows, Anderson saw a group of villagers drawn up along the sandy spit, men and women together, all of them waving and cheering like they'd just won a war or something. Thinking it over, the dark man felt his wry grin returning. Could be they were right, at that.

They'd helped him break up Bradley Gill's bid for power, and see off Lee Sharrock and his guns. Without them, and Ibanez, and Salazar, he would never have had a chance. Same went for Tortuga, Ernesto and the others. Thanks to them, the job was done, and pretty soon he could turn for home again.

Then again, he figured he might have been something of a help himself.

He saw Juana there, standing in the front rank of the crowd. Saw the tall, black-haired woman throw the heavy pistol from her to the ground, running down the beach towards him. Studying that oncoming figure, Anderson smiled wider. He climbed out of the pirogue and stalked through the last few yards of shallow water, going on up the beach to meet her.

Come to think, there was nothing to hurry him right now. It would be days before word reached the nearest federal unit, longer than that before they got round to sending a garrison to the island. Meantime there were wounds to be tended, homes to be rebuilt. A whole community to be restored from the ashes. Least he could do was stay on and help them finish the job.

Walking up the beach to Juana, he

was still smiling. He figured he might even get to like it here.

For a while, anyhow.

THE END